1/14

RED

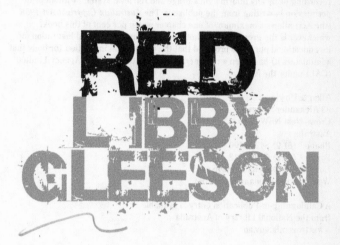

RED
LIBBY GLEESON

ALLEN&UNWIN
SYDNEY · MELBOURNE · AUCKLAND · LONDON

First published in 2012

Allen & Unwin
83 Alexander Street
Crows Nest NSW 2065
Australia
Phone: (61 2) 8425 0100
Fax: (61 2) 9906 2218
Email: info@allenandunwin.com
Web: www.allenandunwin.com

A Cataloguing-in-Publication entry is available
from the National Library of Australia
www.trove.nla.gov.au

ISBN 978 1 74175 853 5

Teachers' notes available from www.allenandunwin.com

Cover and text design by Sandra Nobes
Cover photo by Susan Gordon-Brown (girl) and Steven Siewert (background)
Set in 10½ point Century Old Style by Tou-Can Design
This book was printed in March 2013 at the SOS Print & Media Group,
65 Burrows Road Alexandria, NSW 2015.

10 9 8 7 6

CHAPTER ONE

MUD. IN HER MOUTH, HER NOSE AND HER EYES. MUD IN her hair and caked on her neck and her arms. Mud filling her shoes and seeping through her clothes. She lay sprawled on her side, a garbled, barely distinct sound coming from her: *Jaymartinjaymartin'*. One eye opened, then the other. She coughed, spat, tried to clear her throat. Mud was stuck to her tongue, her gums and the top of her mouth. Still she said the words *Jaymartinjaymartin'*. She tried to sit up, but her left shoulder and arm ached and needle-sharp pain stabbed her fingers, her palms and the backs of her hands. Sand and stones tormented her broken skin.

She fell back. She pushed herself up on her other elbow. *Jaymartinjaymartinjaymartin.'*

Her world was mud and pain.

• • • • •

'What's your name?' A boy was sitting on a kitchen table floating in a muddy pool.

At his feet was a child's doll, the head lolling to one side. Hair as pale as straw hung off the scalp, its eyes loose and drooping.

Jaymartinjaymartin.'

He stepped forward and slapped her hard across the face. 'Shut up that stupid talk.'

She fell sideways, her body shaking. She covered her face with her hands. Light rain was now falling.

He went back to his table.

The girl turned away from him. Screeching seagulls swooped out of the low grey cloud. She heard crashing sounds and voices calling as she dragged herself up onto her knees. Like a swarm of scavenging animals, men were pushing aside planks of wood and sheets of tin. They moved around the broken walls of brick. Then came the roaring, deafening sound of a helicopter, blades whirring, turning above them. Huge up-drafts of wind tossed mud and water flying. What did it mean? What was happening?

He asked her again, 'What's your name?'

'Name?' Her voice was oddly high-pitched like a small child's. *Jaymartinjaymartin*,' she began and then stopped. This time the boy repeated, 'Jaymartin? What do you mean, Jay Martin? James Martin?'

'I don't know.'

'But that's a bloke's name. It can't be yours.'

She spat mud from her mouth. 'Have you got any water? A drink.'

He nodded. 'Water. What a joke.' He held his arms out to the rain. 'At my place. You can come with me, if you like.'

Like? What did he mean? She felt nothing.

She dragged herself free of the mud like someone crawling out of quicksand. She followed him past a wardrobe with the door hanging loose, a cupboard spewing folders and sheets of paper, a couch with its cushions floating on the sea of mud.

Everywhere people were bent over the mounds of brickwork that had been houses. They were pushing aside smashed-up stairs, digging at heaps of battered machinery and twisted metal. Everything tossed and broken.

Over the soft sound of rain came the cry of a lone dog and the constant harsh call of gulls.

●　●　●　●　●

She walked slowly, every muscle in her body screaming out to her to stop. What had done this? Earthquake?

Bombs? She stumbled over mounds of rock and mud, leaning for a moment against a tree trunk torn from the ground.

The boy kept turning his head to look at her. The rain ran down over his head and plastered his straggly brown hair to his back. He led her around more muddy pools, past an upturned boat to his place: the shell of someone's house, roofed with sheets of tin.

'My palace,' he said, and he bowed low as if he was showing off something fantastic. She stepped around the upturned bath and the broken filing cabinet and flopped down onto a sandstone block. Across from her, a car was wedged where a wall had been, as if someone had driven it into the house and then couldn't back it out. The bonnet was crushed and one of the wheels was twisted and buckled.

'That's where I sleep,' the boy said. 'Better than the hard ground.'

He bent to pick up a bowl of water and passed it to her. Ignoring the pain that racked her hands, she gulped it, as if she hadn't drunk for a long time. Some of it splashed down her front.

'You hurt me.' She touched her face where he'd slapped her.

'You were talking rubbish, babbling that name. Who is he?'

'I don't know.'

'What's *your* name?'

'I don't know.'

What was her name? Why was this other one in her head? Jay Martin. James Martin? She started again, softly, saying it over and over.

Whack. The boy came forward and slapped her again.

She fell back.

He seized her elbow and dragged her onto her knees.

'Shut up! Stop your gabbling. You sound crazy. You're gunna have to use your brains.' He squatted, his face in close to her. 'There's lots of people everywhere dead and missing and everything's wrecked.'

She noticed the blue shadow of a bruise down his left cheek.

'What's *your* name?' she whispered.

'Peri.' He drew back from her. 'Sorry about that. I had to get you to shut up. But I'll do it again if you start.' He pulled his wet T-shirt off and wrung it out. 'You've got blood on your arm and you should clean up your hands. Bathroom's over there.' He waved his hand to the opposite brick wall, where buckets filled with water were lined up.

She went slowly across and chose one, scooping up water and splashing it on her face and on her arms. Thin brown trails ran over her pale skin as the caked blood washed away. She poured some of the water into another small bowl and soaked her hands. Peri came and crouched beside her. 'Looks like you put up a fight against a barbed-wire fence.'

Slowly, wincing, she washed dirt and sand from the cuts and torn patches of skin.

'You've got blood too.' She pointed to his knuckles and an angry slash across his hand.

'Nah, it's nothing.'

When she had finished she sat back on the block of stone and blew on her aching fingers. 'Where is everyone? Why is everything wrecked? What happened? Where are we?'

'Well, it is Sydney, though it doesn't look like it. I dunno what this suburb was. It rained and it rained,' he said. 'I saw on this big screen last night that they reckon there was this cyclone like the ones they get up north. It was out at sea and then it turned and huge waves came roaring up over the beaches and the land and it just took everything for nearly a kilometre. It never happened like that before, not round here. There're lots of people dead or missing and injured and everything's smashed up. The army's been called in to rescue people, and the SES.' He paused. 'There were some people, police and rescue mobs, came through yesterday and I reckon there'll soon be a whole gang of soldiers. Be good. Get rid of some of the scavengers.'

'Who?'

'Those people we saw. They're just looking for stuff so they can make some money.'

'Maybe they used to live there. Maybe that was their smashed house.'

'I reckon all the people in the house would be dead under the rubble or washed out to sea.'

'Why wasn't I washed out?' Her voice trailed away. Shivers ran from her chest, down her arms to her hands till her whole body was shaking. She couldn't stop. She drew her knees up and wrapped her arms around them, entwining her fingers despite the pain from her cuts and torn skin. Backwards and forwards she rocked, teeth chattering. Who had she been with? What happened to them? Was it her mum or dad? Brothers or sisters?

She took a deep breath and slowly steadied herself. 'What will the soldiers do? Will they help us?'

He shrugged.

'Do they take you somewhere?'

'Probably to a shelter.'

'What's that?'

'Kind of like a hospital.'

'I don't need a hospital.' She touched the back of her head. 'But my head really hurts. And my hands are a mess.'

'Are you sure you don't know what your name is? What I can call you?' said Peri.

She thought for a minute. Nothing. There was nothing in her head but a small voice and that name she kept repeating.

'I don't know. I can't remember.'

'You must have a name. What about that Martin person you were jabbering on about. Is he your father?'

'I don't know. It's like words in my head. It's all I know.'

Her father? Was he? How could she know her father's name but not her own? Who was he? What did he look like? And her mother? What about her? She frowned, trying to summon a picture.

She fell silent. Empty. Unconnected.

'Where is he? Was he with you?'

'I don't know.' She stood up and moved to lean against the car.

'What about you?' she said. 'Where's your family?'

'Haven't got one. Don't need one.' He picked up a stick and scratched at the dirt at his feet. 'My family's all gone. This is where I live now.'

Was hers all gone too? How could she not know? What did she know? She looked down at her hands. These are hands. These are fingers, knuckles, wrists, arms. I know stuff. I'm not stupid. But who am I?

'I've got some food,' Peri said. 'Are you hungry?'

She nodded. When had she last eaten? What had she last eaten?

She watched him climb into the car and come back with slices of bread and some fruit. He broke a banana into small pieces and handed her the sandwich he made with it. He held out a cup of water and she filled her mouth and rinsed off mud and salt-tasting sand.

'It's not exactly a top restaurant,' he said.

'It's good.' She ate hungrily, squashing the soft fruit between her teeth, feeling it take into her stomach the last little bits of grit.

'How did you get that bruise on your face? I thought you said you weren't in all the mess.'

'I wasn't.'

'So?'

'So mind your own business.'

When they'd finished she looked at him and said simply, 'I don't know what to do.'

'You can stay here if you like.'

'Stay with you?'

'Have you got a better idea? You can sleep in the car.'

'But I need to find out who I am. Maybe someone is looking for me. I must have a family out there.'

'You don't need a family. You can be all right on your own.'

She shook her head. She felt lost, alone.

'I could show you where there's one of those kind of hospital places.'

'What for? I'm not sick. There must be somewhere else.'

He shrugged. 'There's a rescue centre where they give out food and blankets and stuff like that. It's OK but you have to steer clear of the cops. They might want to put you somewhere for lost kids. You know, like a kids' home. There're loads of kids wandering around. They're everywhere. And they might grab me too.'

'What's wrong with that?'

'I'm not getting bossed around by anyone. That's what happens in places like that. They make you do stuff that you don't want to do, and if you don't do it they whack you.'

They were quiet for a while. The rain had stopped and the girl felt her sore limbs warm in the sun. She rolled her shoulders, wincing a little from the pain, then stretched out her legs and flexed her ankles.

'If you don't know your name,' said Peri, 'we should make one up just so I can call you something.'

'Like what?'

'I dunno.'

'Have you got a mum or a sister? I could borrow their name.'

He looked away.

'What did you think when you first saw me?'

'I thought you were dead.'

'Well, that won't work as a name.'

'I saw your bright red T-shirt in the mud and I went over to see what it was. I could call you Red.'

'Sounds like dead. Try other words that mean red.'

'Rose. Scarlet. Ruby.'

Rose? That felt familiar. Ruby? She felt she knew the word but as she tried to grasp the thought it darted from her mind, like a little fish zipping through water.

'What's a ruby?'

'You know. A jewel. A bright red jewel. Like rich people wear.'

She looked at her torn, mud-stained T-shirt. 'That's not me.'

'I'm just gunna call you Red. I reckon you might even have red hair – under all that mud.'

'Suit yourself.' She closed her eyes. Her head hurt. Her hands hurt. She wanted to think about what had happened but it was too hard. Later. She'd think later.

'That place where they give out the food,' said Peri, 'I could just sneak in and get stuff. I've done that before.'

'But how does that help me find out who I am?'

'Worry about that when you get more food in your belly. And you need some clothes. I have to get more water too. This rainwater won't last and all the pipes are wrecked. The sewers are leaking everywhere.'

She looked down at her mud-encrusted jeans. No running water. No washing. No clean clothes. No toilets. Nothing to drink. No one to turn to. Suddenly she could feel every bit of her body. It was as if all of her flesh was squeezing her stomach, pressing in on it and then moving away to leave only a shell, an emptiness. Her hands were shaking.

'This is crazy. We can't live like this, on our own. We need to go and find someone to help us. We have to.'

'No way.'

'Why can't we go to the police or the soldiers?'

''Cos we can't.' He was yelling at her now, his face red and frowning. 'People say they'll help you but they just want to control you and tell you what to do.' He turned away from her, mumbling something, pressing his hands down into the pockets of his jeans.

'Sor-ry.' Her voice came out as a whisper.

'I'll go to the Centre. You stay here,' he said. 'It'll be quicker if I go by myself.'

He walked off. She watched him growing smaller and smaller till he disappeared. Why was she staying here, doing what he said? And why wasn't he with *his* family? What had happened to them?

A seagull cawed overhead, swooped around in a wide arc and came down to land only a metre from her. Red leant forward. Another gull flew in and then another. They tottered towards her on their skinny red legs. 'Ruby legs,' she whispered. 'Sorry. I've got nothing to feed you.' Nothing to feed myself.

• • • • •

The afternoon dragged on. The clouds had disappeared and Red moved every so often to follow the sun. Heat in the stones dried her jeans and the warmth relaxed her sore muscles. Then it became too hot and she moved herself into a spot where the remaining bits of the wall cast a cooler shadow. She looked out over the shattered landscape. The scavengers were gone. I am the only person in the world. Despite the heat, she shivered. She looked down at the dirt at her feet. A line of ants marched out from under a fallen sandstone block, turned right at the edge of a pile of bricks and disappeared back under a fallen wooden beam. They knew where to go. What if Peri didn't come back? What if someone did grab him and stopped him from coming? What if the rain started again and more waves came and reached in to her and destroyed this place? What if...what if...Her body was shaking again. She slumped forward and tears welled in her eyes. What if...At her feet were crushed leaves stuck in pockets of muddy water. Fallen from their branch, adrift. That's me. Come back, Peri, come back. Stop it. Stop these thoughts. You are alive. He has found you and fed you and he has promised to come back.

● ● ● ● ●

She sat up and ran her thumbs through her salty hair, trying to break up the muddy clumps. Her skin was dry and itchy. She scratched her back and neck. Her fingers brushed against a leather cord. She pulled at it and from under her T-shirt came a long, looping strand

and on the end of it a solid metal tube. She spat on it and rubbed it clean. Smooth metal locket. Who had given it to her? Did she always wear it?

Was this a clue to who she was? She gripped the locket tightly, ignoring the pain in her hands.

She wanted Peri to return. She stood up and saw him picking his way over the slabs of broken concrete. She waved and called out, 'Peri, Peri.' Then as he came closer, she felt silly and she stepped back into the shadow and was silent as he came up to her.

'What did you get?'

'Food. There's enough fruit for a few days and they had packets of stuff – special rations that soldiers have. There's even chocolate. And I scrounged a backpack and I got you some clothes.'

He shook out a bag on the ground. Coloured T-shirts, men's and boys' style, landed at her feet. 'I had to say they were for me,' he grinned and waved his hand over his skinny chest. 'You're nearly as big as me. I reckon they'll fit you.' He sat down. 'Any visitors while I was away?'

She shook her head. 'As if. I found this, though. I was wearing it round my neck.' She passed him the locket.

'Weird,' he whispered. It lay flat on his palm. He stroked it with the fingers of his other hand, turned it over and traced a tiny ridge along the top. 'It might open. There might be something inside.' He scratched it with his thumbnail. 'Pity we haven't got a knife or something sharp.'

'Couldn't we ask at the centre?' said Red. 'We should go in there anyway. There must be records and people looking for other people. Someone must know me. I'm not some freak from another planet.'

Peri shrugged. 'It's crazy, Red. Nobody's got time for a kid like you. They're putting up tents but there are way too many people. All their computers are down and there are piles and piles of clothes and toys but only a few people to hand them out and everyone's sticking up photos of relatives they've lost and there are reporters and cops and everyone's going totally wild.' He passed the locket back to Red. 'We can go back there tomorrow but if you want to find out who you are, I reckon you'll have to do it yourself.'

CHAPTER TWO

IT GREW DARKER. PERI WRENCHED OPEN THE DOORS OF the car.

'You can have the back seat if you like. I'll take the front.'

Red curled up on the cracked plastic, her head on the door's armrest. She smelt fungus and decay. In the mud on the floor was orange peel and screwed-up bags that had once held takeaway food: the smell of stale pizza slices, hamburgers, tomato sauce and cold fat lingered.

Through the broken back window of the car, the stars were vague and indistinct, half covered with streaks of cloud. She stared at them, wishing she could identify them in some way, to know them. Eventually her eyes closed and she fell into a troubled sleep.

• • • • •

In the morning, over a handful of dried apricots and chocolate, she said, 'I want to go back and look around where you found me.'

'Why? There's no one left out there,' Peri said. 'When I found you I'd been all round that part.'

'I still want to see it,' she said quietly. 'It might make me remember something. And I want to go to the Centre and see the photos on the wall. Someone in my family might have been away for the day. My mum or my dad, they might have been at work in the city or visiting somewhere else. They could be desperate, going crazy looking for me right now.'

'OK, but I'm telling you, you won't find anything.'

They shared a packet of biscuits, crisp tasteless squares, and a bottle of strangely flavoured juice. 'It's what they have for soldiers,' said Peri. 'You can't buy this in shops. It's full of everything you need to stay alive in a battle zone. Protein and stuff. Another good reason not to join the army.' He grinned. 'They're opening up all the emergency stuff they keep for when there's a war.' He wiped his face with the back of his hand. 'It's just like that out there. There are soldiers and police all over the place and tanks and army tents. And everywhere looks as though it's been bombed.'

• • • • •

They retraced their steps to the place where Peri had found her. 'I used to swim at the next beach down that way.' He waved his hand to the south. 'The cliff collapsed there in the storm. You'd have to be a mad dog to swim there now.'

'And all those houses are wrecked or gone,' said Red.

They scrambled over the rubble, the smashed furniture and the dead and broken trees. She could hear the sea, the low, even murmuring of the water washing itself against the land. Then she saw it. Far in the distance the clear blue of the sky rubbed up against the duller blue-green of the ocean. Closer in, its colour changed to the brown of floating tree branches, timber and mud. Each crashing wave dumped more rubbish on the narrow strip of land.

She couldn't take her eyes away. The sound, the rhythm, the feeling…she was being picked up, rolled over, dumped, water above her. Water below her, pushing her on and down.

She was shaking. Tears streamed down her face. Her chest tightened. She gulped and forced herself to turn around, to put the sea behind her.

'Did you hear what I said?' Peri frowned. 'There used to be an unreal beach down there.' He pointed. 'In the olden days there was about a hundred metres of sand when the tide was out. Kids used to surf 'cos it had the best waves. Sand's all gone now. Once I met this old bloke who said that when he was a kid they used to have big carnivals at the beach. Hundreds of surf lifesavers and kids too, all competing for prizes. Swimming, boat racing and marching. He'd said he had photos to prove it and one day he'd bring them down and show me but he never did.'

'Maybe I lived in a house around here.' Red was trying to talk normally. She turned to right and left, her eyes skimming over the mounds of mud and bricks, timber, lumps of concrete, wire, furniture and toys. A shimmering blue party dress, the skirt torn into dangling shreds, hung from the upturned roots of a Moreton Bay fig tree.

'Or you could've been just visiting.'

They slowly picked their way back. Part of Red wanted to search under every scrap of debris but another part felt sure there was nothing to find. She kicked at a pile of bricks under sheets of iron. Black flies shot up like an exploding firework. She saw a swollen, rotting animal, its matted hair, distorted face. Someone's dog. A putrid smell. Red's stomach leapt to her throat. She stumbled forward and knelt in the mud as acrid-tasting vomit poured from her mouth.

The smells of dead and rotting grass, stagnant pools and the foul water leaking from broken pipes hung all around her.

'Let's get out of here,' she said.

• • • • •

Back at the 'palace', Peri put the remaining food into the backpack. Red rinsed her mouth and sorted through the new clothes, choosing a pair of pale cotton shorts and a bright yellow T-shirt with a foot-ball logo.

'Don't turn round,' she said as she pulled her red top over her head. Her mud-soaked jeans were harder to take off. She undid the top and rolled the stiffened fabric slowly down over her thighs. The gashes on her hands still stung. Blue-green bruises covered both her knees and were scattered over her shins. She pulled on the T-shirt and shorts and brushed at the dirt on her legs. The clothes were big on her but she felt freer, more able to move.

'If you had really short hair, you'd look like a boy,' said Peri.

'Thanks a lot.' She felt there was something clever she should say but it was too hard to come up with it. 'Are you going to come with me?'

He shrugged. 'I'll take you there. Got nothing else to do.'

• • • • •

At the rescue centre there were mountains of clothes and toys, and piles of books and kitchen things. Everywhere were people: family groups with little kids clutching at their parents' knees, couples with arms entwined, and bigger kids wandering as if they had nowhere to belong. Old people were sitting, hunched on the odd square of bare grass or in the shade of trees, fanning themselves with pages torn from a magazine.

And noise. Calling out, shouting and crying. Voices buzzed above the sound of the rumbling of generators, the grinding of the gears of slow-moving vehicles and the screech of sirens.

'Come on.' Peri grabbed at her arm.

'There're too many people.' Red's voice suddenly stuck in her throat.

'That's good,' said Peri. 'No one'll take much notice of us.'

Red shivered. She wanted someone to notice her, to know her.

'Come on. You're the one who wanted to see this, not me.' Peri pulled her with him. She followed him like an obedient child.

Peri fought his way through to the biggest building.

Around one side, a door led into the main hall. Boards covered with photographs and scribbled messages lined the walls. People swarmed in front of them, some silent, their eyes scanning quickly, others gasping and putting their hands up to cover their faces, their bodies slumped, defeated.

'So many,' whispered Red. 'I'll never get to look at all of them. I don't even know what I'm looking for.'

'I'll start from the far end and meet you in the middle,' said Peri. 'Just see if anyone is looking for a girl of about eleven or twelve, reddish-brown hair, a few freckles, pretty ordinary-looking.'

'Thanks a lot.'

She watched him walk quickly away from her. This was so weird. Why was he doing this? One minute he wanted to help, the next he didn't care. And who was he?

● ● ● ● ●

Red's first picture was a woman in a swimming costume holding a naked toddler. She was pointing at the camera, grinning, while he was squinting into the sun. *My daughter and grandson* was scrawled underneath and then a phone number, names and an address. Red moved on. People of every colour and age were there: old men and women with faces leathered by years in the sun, grinning surfers, laughing children, men and women holding chuckling infants and babies. Each had beneath it a name, an age and a possible last place where the person was known to have lived or worked or been visiting. Some images showed whole families in front of their beachfront houses. Then there were no pictures, just lists of names. Red moved more and more slowly, weighed down by the disappeared. How could she know if any of these people belonged to her? She didn't have a name, a face to claim as her own. Her stomach, her throat, her whole body felt empty, lost. If she wasn't on this board, did that mean no one missed her, there was no one to claim her? Did she belong to no one?

Peri met her in the middle.

'There's no photo of you,' he said, 'and nothing that sounds like you.' He reached out and touched her shoulder.

She nodded. 'Not so far here either but I still need to keep looking.'

'What's the point?' he said.

'I have to.' She pulled away from him and moved on along the boards that he had checked.

She stopped in front of a smiling couple sitting on a stone fence, with the sea in the background. Could they be her parents? What if they were? The sun was bouncing off the water and he had his arm across her shoulders, one finger playing with the dolphin-shaped earring that dangled below her hair. Then she read what was scribbled underneath: *My daughter and her husband. Their baby was with me at my home when the sea came in*. Red didn't bother to read the numbers and details that followed. She moved on. A man smiled down from a glossy photo. Under his signature was written: *Well-known star of television and film, believed to be lost from his home in Coogee.* Could he be her father? A couple, sitting on the grass under a sign that read BRONTE BEACH. What about them?

A woman was standing staring at the photo as tears streamed down her face. A weeping toddler clung to her leg. The woman's hand touched the child's hair but everything about her was elsewhere. The child turned and looked up at Red. His little face was streaked with dirt and tears. He opened his mouth as wide as possible and began to scream, louder and louder. At first the mother looked as if she didn't care and then she scooped him up in her arms and holding him tightly to her chest pushed her way through the crowds to the door.

Red gazed at photo after photo and then came to another board with scrawled messages in large black writing.

Taryn, I'm safe and at Mum's out in Concord. Call me.

Found – Black cat with name Tinkerbelle on neck tag. Call me 0465423319.

Emergency accommodation in Christian home, call 9457666.

It began to blur. She was staring at the boards but the words no longer meant anything. She was alone, wading through a fog or a world made of mud thin enough to allow her to move but so thick as to hide the real world from her.

Peri grabbed her shoulder. 'Are you all right? You look like you're about to fall over.'

'I have to get out of here.'

He pushed through the crowd. They made it to the door, where they stood for a moment, Red gulping down huge mouthfuls of air.

Voices were coming from beyond the gardens. At first they could just be heard above the general sound of the crowd. Then they became louder and louder.

'Get out. Get out!' a man was screaming. 'You're just mongrels feeding off us.' Red saw his arms waving and pushing at the camera and at the reporter who held a microphone and other sound equipment. More people gathered, some throwing punches at the media staff, some trying to hold back the screaming man. Red and Peri stared. The man had slumped on the grass. Another man knelt beside him, and put an arm across his shoulders. The camera was still filming.

'Poor guy,' whispered Red. 'He probably lost everything too.'

They moved out into the grounds and squatted on the damp grass.

'Are you OK?' Peri said.

She shrugged. 'I don't know what OK is any more.' She rubbed the sore spot on the back of her head. 'I'm here, I'm alive, but my head is a big black hole. There's nothing there. It's empty. Who am I, Peri? Who am I?'

He shrugged but said nothing.

They sat for a while, staring at a couple of young children playing with a ball. They were running and laughing, tossing the ball high in the air and pushing each other trying to be the one to catch it. A tired-looking older woman kept her eye on them, staring with fierce concentration as if to look away would be to lose them.

'We could put a sign up in there,' said Red. 'I could write a description and we could stick it on the board.'

'Better if we had a photo.' Peri stood up. 'There must be someone with a phone and a printer.'

'I don't want to go back in there.'

'Come on, you're the one who wanted to come here in the first place. You have to,' he said.

● ● ● ● ●

In a side room, a smiling young woman in a Salvation Army uniform handed them pen and paper.

'Who are you looking for?'

'Jay Martin,' said Red.

'What does *J* stand for?'

'James Martin,' said Peri.

'And is he your father?'

Peri nodded.

'And your mother?'

'She's dead,' said Peri. 'But not in all this. She died a long time ago.'

'I am sorry.' She took out her camera and waved Red and Peri to stand close together.

'I thought this was just for me,' whispered Red.

'Shh, she thinks we're brother and sister. Let her. It means no more questions.'

'We aren't, are we?'

'Don't be stupid. You may have forgotten who you are but I haven't.'

The woman passed them the sheet of paper from the printer. Peri took it and wrote: *Looking for our father James Martin, maybe lost in Bronte area. Leave message here*.

'You need to put your names,' said the woman.

Peri hesitated for a moment and then wrote *Ruby Martin* and *Peri Martin*.

Red took the photo from him. They were not like brother and sister: her hair short, curly and red-brown, his long and straggling almost to his shoulders. His face was thin and sun-tanned, hers round and pale and scattered with a sprinkling of freckles.

'Where are you staying?' asked the woman.

'With friends,' said Peri. 'But we might be moving, so we'll just come in here tomorrow and in a few days to see if he's been.'

'Are you sure you two are all right?'

Peri nodded. 'We're fine.'

Outside in the sun Red said, 'Why did you say that? We aren't fine.' She dropped down onto the straggly grass. 'I don't know who I am, and we don't know whether James Martin is my dad. We don't even know that that is his name and we've told them you're my brother and you aren't. You don't look anything like me. No one's going to recognise me from that photo and we don't have anywhere to stay.'

'We do. The palace is fine. We've put up that sign and that's the best we can do so far.'

'And I'm hungry.'

Peri pulled her to her feet. 'Quit whingeing. Let's go over the road. Look.'

A RED CROSS DISASTER RELIEF banner was hanging from an upstairs window of the building across the road. It half covered a sign saying ...LY HIGH SCHOOL. There were more people than there had been at the centre. Huge green army marquees and smaller tents covered a football field. Groups gathered in the yard, the gardens and in the courtyard. Arrows directed them to the canteen where large pots were set out on benches. Peri and Red joined a queue that moved slowly forward towards a woman, her dress pulled tight across her chest, sitting at a table. She said, 'Where are your coupons?'

'Our mums have got them,' said Peri.

'Where are they?'

'Back there.' He nodded to where the queue stretched almost to the fence.

'I can't serve you without a coupon.'

'We're hungry,' said Peri. 'We've been at the other place and then they sent us here and now our mums are talking back there and...'

'Oh, all right then, take it.'

She passed them each a plate of beans in a rich tomato sauce.

'You are such a liar,' said Red as they moved across the grass.

'Gets us fed,' he grinned.

● ● ● ● ●

When they had finished, Red said, 'Is your mum really dead?'

Peri nodded.

'And your dad?'

'He's alive.'

'Why don't you live with him, then?'

''Cos I don't.'

'But at least you've got a dad...'

'I don't want to talk about it.'

'But...'

'I said I don't want to talk about it.'

CHAPTER THREE

THEY WERE ALMOST BACK AT THE PALACE. PERI STOPPED, his hand on Red's shoulder. Ahead of them on the roof of the car was a boy with something in his hand.

'Who's that?' said Red.

'You don't want to know,' said Peri. 'Stay here.' He bent down, picked up a stone and moved on ahead of her.

The boy on the car raised a metal bar. *Smash*, he whacked it through the front windscreen. *Smash*, the side window went.

'Quit it!' Peri hurled the stone at the boy, who ducked and screamed and swung the bar above his head. Peri was running now, leaping over the rocks and the rubble towards the palace.

'Ya gunna make me?' yelled the boy. 'This is my place now. Get 'im.'

Peri stopped. Four boys were leaning against the last bit of wall next to the upturned water buckets. They each picked up bits of brick. A chunk of mortar whizzed past Peri's ear, another struck his shoulder.

Peri stepped back and waved to Red. She turned and ran.

She heard the boy on the car screaming and she glanced back over her shoulder. He leapt to the bonnet and then the ground. Metal bar held high, he charged at Peri.

For a moment Peri held his ground, then, with five boys bearing down on him, he turned and ran after Red. She was running as fast as she could, gasping for breath, grabbing air into her mouth. There were footsteps pounding behind her and she hoped they were Peri's. This time she dared not look. Her chest hurt and she stumbled and almost fell as her feet slipped in the mud.

'Keep going, Red,' yelled Peri.

On and on she ran, down streets with the bitumen torn up and broken, through a caryard full of vehicles tossed on their sides like a pod of beached whales, till she reached a children's playground.

She looked back over her shoulder. Peri was almost level with her. No one was following them. She stopped, clasping her chest and puffing. She dropped onto a swing, the only structure still standing. 'Who *was* that?'

Peri shook his head and bent over, his chest heaving. After a moment he straightened up. 'I don't know his name. He thinks he's king around here. I had a fight with him yesterday, but he didn't have his mates then.'

'So that's where your bruises came from.'

He nodded.

'It's not fair. That was your place.'

Peri shrugged. 'You get used to it. Nothing lasts. You have to move on.'

She pushed her feet against the damp grass till the swing rocked gently back and forward. 'So what do we do now? Where are we going to sleep?'

Peri didn't answer for a few minutes. He just stood there till his breathing became normal.

'Maybe we should go back to the Centre,' said Red. 'At least there we can get food and there might be room in a tent or something.'

Peri shook his head. 'I know a better place. Follow me.'

She slid off the swing reluctantly and fell into step beside him. The two of them walked in silence for about ten minutes. They were moving further away from the sea and the shells of buildings, past rows of houses. Some fences were gone, windows and doors were smashed and in one case a whole side wall had collapsed. That left the inside of the house like the cut-away of an ants' nest: a glance showed a girl's bedroom with a purple cover half over the bed, a desk piled high with books and papers, a red-and-white sundress on the floor with sandals and other shoes, mugs, CD covers and magazines. Red wondered did she too have a room like this? Peri urged her on.

People stood on the road or in their yards, talking in small groups, pointing out the parts of their damaged homes. One man had two suitcases stuffed as if ready to go on summer holidays. He held a laptop and folders to his chest like a barrier against the world. It was eerily quiet.

Red and Peri reached the open green of an oval covered in shredded branches and leaves, paper, timber and sheets of roofing iron. Peri kept walking but something made Red stop. Had she been here before? Was this place familiar? She felt she was digging through rubble to find memories.

'Come on,' called Peri. They were at the entrance to a primary school. Blue-and-white police tape wound its way around the whole site. A huge sign lay broken and twisted on the cracked cement path. Doors and windows were gone, mud and sand was washed a metre high against the walls and the corner of the whole block had sunk into spongy ground.

Peri ducked under the tape. 'Our next home,' he said. 'This one's big enough to be a real palace.'

Red followed him, picking her way across the broken path, stepping over tree branches and collapsed fence posts. 'Was this your school?'

He shook his head. 'No way. I don't come from round here. Look, we can get in there.' He pointed to a doorway that led into a block on the far side of a quadrangle. Inside, a hall doubled as a gym. Stage curtains were half ripped from the ceiling and toppled equipment, goalposts and floor-mats had been washed hard up against a far wall. Red and Peri were standing ankle-deep in muddy sand and there was an overwhelming smell of rot and mould.

'I'm not sleeping in here,' Red screwed up her nose. 'There must be somewhere else we can go, upstairs, a classroom or a library or something.'

They went back outside. The sun had disappeared behind one of the buildings and shadows now crept across the quadrangle. They crossed the yard to the canteen where a bright red sign, *Healthy body = healthy mind*, lay buckled in the doorway. A wide cement stairwell led to the top floor. Inside, banks of computers lined the walls and rows of freestanding shelves were filled with books. On the wall behind the librarian's desk was a poster about opening hours and fines and next to that a series of huge photographs. Hundreds of students, all in navy-blue uniforms, their faces shining in the sunlight, smiled up at the camera. Behind them stood rows of teachers with arms folded.

Red walked between the shelves. Nonfiction: 994–999 Australian History: *Convicts in Australia*, *The Life of Bennelong*, *Too Many Captain Cooks*. 780–789 Music, 641–649 Cooking, 620–629 Transport. At least I can still read. Under the far window was a cluster of beanbags. She pushed herself down into one, squirming and enjoying the feeling of the tiny beads massaging her tired body. She had to think. Think about who she was. Who she belonged to. Jay Martin. James Martin. Maybe John Martin or Joseph Martin. Who was he? How could she find out?

Peri flopped into a bag alongside her. 'Not a bad place,' he said. 'We could hole up here for ages.'

'We can't eat books.'

'There's probably tinned and packet stuff in the canteen, but. And there could be drinks and lollies. I'll go down and have a look.'

'It might all be wrecked.'

'Might not.' He got up then and headed for the door. 'You want to come with me?'

She shook her head.

Whenever Peri wasn't with her, her mind was a big, empty space. She tried to fill it up with faces: people she'd seen in the past twenty-four hours, images of the missing from the giant boards of photographs at the Centre. The weeping, screaming child. The woman he was with looked like his mother but had he lost his dad? Had she, Red? Someone was her mum, her dad. She pressed her eyes tightly together. I'm going crazy. Do something. She stood up and wandered back through the rows of books. Nonfiction. Reference dictionaries, puzzles, word games. She crossed into a different section. Novels. Thick fantasy paperbacks with gold lettering and dark dragon figures leaping off the spines. Then she was at a smaller shelf, low down so she had to kneel to see the slim, square volumes facing outwards. Picture books. She picked out a thicker book and sat down on the floor.

Grimm's Fairy Tales. The cover had a pale image of a woman in a long mauve gown leaning towards a knight in steel-grey armour. Red put the book on her lap and let it fall open. 'Hansel and Gretel.' Once upon a time there were two children, Hansel and Gretel. She stopped reading. She knew this. She closed her eyes. This is the story of the children left by themselves in the forest. The wicked stepmother. The woodcutter father. The house made of lollies. The wicked witch who wants to eat Hansel but Gretel pushes her into the oven. Red rocked backwards and forwards. How do I know this? Have I read it before or has someone read this to me? Has someone told it to me? Who?

Another book caught her eye. A slim volume, it had no rich colours, no huge bright letters or bold illustration. The cover was plain and simple: white background and a black line drawing of a girl. Short, untidy hair, T-shirt. It was roughly done in charcoal or crayon and the face, the huge dark eyes were staring straight at the viewer. Red felt she was looking at herself.

She was about to open it when she heard a noise at the door. Peri came into the room, his arms bursting with cans, packets of pasta and bottles of juice.

Red quickly pushed the book under the shelf, ignoring the pain in her fingers as they scraped the hard cover.

Chocolate bars poked from Peri's pocket. 'Look at all this. We won't starve.' He dumped everything on the librarian's desk. 'And I've even found this.' He held up a tin-opener.

Red came over to him and looked at the tins. 'Tomatoes, tuna, baked beans. You're right, we won't starve. You're a good thief.' She took a chocolate bar and pulled off the wrapper.

'Years of practice.'

'Is that how you survive? I mean, where *have* you been living? And where were you when the cyclone came?'

Peri pushed himself up onto the desk. 'I was living in this big old warehouse, a couple of kilometres away.

There were other kids there too. Sometimes when it was real hot we slept down on the beach. The roof got blown off right at the start of the winds. Then the rain came in. We headed out then. I slept in a church the night when the waves came.' He pointed to the beanbags. 'Not as good as this, though.'

Red shook her head. Sleeping in a church. Had she ever done that? Could she have? She pushed the question from her mind. Here she was, about to sleep in a school.

Peri busied himself sorting the packets and tins into separate piles. 'What have you been doing?'

Red shrugged. 'Not much. Reading a bit. It's weird, I don't know who I am but when this book opened at "Hansel and Gretel" I knew it. I remembered it from somewhere.'

'Hansel and Gretel?'

'You know, the one where the kids are left out in the forest by the father and the wicked stepmother.'

'Hmm.'

'What?'

'Nothing.'

'And then they find the witch's house made of gingerbread and lollies.'

Peri waved a bag of jellybeans in the air. 'Like us, eh? Only we haven't got the witch, at least not with us at the moment.' He tore open the bag and dropped a couple of the lollies into his mouth.

'Sometimes I feel a bit like I'm in a story that someone's made up and they're moving me around and maybe they're going to let me find out who I am and who that Jay or James Martin is. I wish I knew how it would end.'

Peri slid off the desk. He stood for a moment in front of the photos.

'Red. Have you had a look at these?' He was peering intently at one of the large images of the whole school, running his finger backwards and forwards along the rows of faces.

'No. Why?'

'There's a girl here in the second row and I reckon it might be you.'

CHAPTER FOUR

'THAT IS YOU,' PERI POINTED TO A GIRL IN THE BACK
row, sitting next to the one holding the sign. *Year Five*.

Red stared at the photograph. Was that really her?
Head tilted back, a huge grin on her face. Someone
must have said something funny. Just ordinary-
looking. Ginger hair cut short, same height as all the
others, same blue shirt with the white logo of a tree
on her chest.

'Two years ago,' said Peri. 'Let's check the others.'

She was there again in the photo for the year
before. This time she had a fringe straggling into her
eyes and a ponytail over her left shoulder.

'That's you all right,' said Peri. 'What about last year? Year Six.'

Nothing. They ran their fingers along the faces. The same grins and clusters of friends. This time a boy held the sign. Red felt the pushing and the shoving, the desperate feeling of wanting to be with a best friend, there in the photo, the photographer cracking a joke, urging them to 'Say cheese' but the kids saying 'Sex', preserved like an experiment. Forever.

Only she wasn't there.

'Maybe you were sick,' said Peri, 'or jigging school. That's why I'm not in school photos.'

Red shook her head. Without thinking she said, 'I wasn't there because I wasn't at this school any more.' Where had that come from? Where had she been?

'How come?' said Peri.

'I don't know. That just came out of my mouth.' Red closed her eyes and rolled her head back. 'I don't know anything any more.'

They munched chocolate and jellybeans in silence for a while. Then Peri said, 'If you were at this school you must be in their records somewhere.'

'What do you mean?'

'Well, everyone has a number and a record that has on it who they are and who their parents are, where they live and what they've done at school and everything.'

'Really? How do you know that?'

'I always got into trouble at school. When Dad got called in to talk to the teachers they had all these printouts of results and when I hadn't been there. Just about down to every time I farted.'

'You mean, on the computer?'

He nodded.

'But there's no electricity, no power.'

'Mmm. Yeah. Maybe a computer will run long enough on batteries to give us what we want.'

'And maybe you know the password to this school's computers.'

'Good point.'

Peri opened the cupboard under the photographs. He pulled out magazines and papers and flicked through them.

'What are you doing? What're you looking for?'

'Some schools have magazines or newsletters and things that have pictures of kids doing stuff. You could be in one.'

'It'd have to be an old one.'

'Lots of librarians hoard the ones left over.'

'How do you know all this?'

Peri grinned. 'I've been to a few schools in my time.'

Red joined him on the floor. They made piles of the catalogues of books and library and computer furniture. They found newsletters filled with information for parents and sometimes a photo of a presentation or an exhibition of student artwork. Nothing was more than six months old.

'You're not here,' said Peri, 'After Year Five, you don't exist.'

• • • • •

It grew darker. They found more beanbags scattered around the library and made a nest for themselves under the window.

'I could read you a story,' said Red. 'Put you to sleep.'

'Weird. No one's ever done that for me before.'

'Or I could tell one.' Red sat deep in her bag and tucked her knees up under her chin. 'Once upon a time there was a famous actor called James Martin and he lived near the coast and he had a boat and he used to go out sailing everywhere and sometimes he'd go with his family and sometimes he'd go by himself and one day he went out and he didn't know it but there was a big cyclone coming and his family thought he was dead but what they didn't know was that his boat got washed all the way in onto the land and he got tossed out and he hit his head and he couldn't remember who he was and so he wandered around for a while till he got better and then he remembered that he had a daughter and he had to find out if she was all right and so he went to the Centre to see if she was there.'

'And was she?'

'No. But she'd put her photo up and every day she'd come to see if her dad was there and one day they found each other.'

'And what happened then?'

'They lived happily ever after.'

'It won't be like that, Red. You're kidding yourself.'

'It's just a story.'

'Maybe.'

'And anyway, I want to go back to that place, the Centre, and look in the morning.'

● ● ● ● ●

Red woke early. Peri still slept, stretched out on the floor where he'd rolled from his beanbag.

She pushed herself up and moved quietly across to the window. Pink morning light washed over the courtyard below her. She flicked a layer of dead flies off the sill and stared down at the seats around the stump of a fallen tree. Did I sit there? Is that where I ate my lunch? With friends? Why can't I remember them? And why aren't I in that final photo? She went back to the librarian's desk and stared at the photos. She tried to put names to the kids who were standing around her. The girl next to her in Year Five with curly black hair and her arm in a sling. Had she broken it at school when Red was there? Were they all playing on the monkey-bars or racing round the playground and she fell? Or the one holding the sign. She was shorter than the others but she had the biggest grin. Is that why they gave her the sign? What was her name?

Red wandered into a side room off the main part of the library. More computers lined walls that were covered with posters: *Join the Reading Challenge*, *Defeat Bullying, Celebrate Diversity* and *Love Your Library*. Desks were set in a horseshoe shape, ready for a discussion group. Red picked up a backpack lying on the floor. She flipped it to see if it was empty. Two blackened bananas fell to the floor.

She took the pack out to the main desk and put into it some of the food that Peri had found, drinks and chocolate bars. Then she went over to the book-shelf. She slid the book with the haunting face of the girl out from where she had hidden it. Why had she done that? She stuffed the book into the pack without looking at it.

Peri was stirring. 'You're up early.' He rolled onto his stomach and rested his chin in his hands. 'What are we going to do today?'

'The Centre,' said Red. 'I want to see if anyone has written on our photo. I know it's crazy, there won't be anything, but I just have to know.' She tossed an energy bar to him. 'That's breakfast.'

They walked along the top corridor and down the

internal staircase. Stories and poems were Blu-tacked to the wall. Red didn't linger to read.

They cut across the oval where the grass was ankle-deep and they had to step between the bits of rubbish strewn around. The sun was hot and the glare from it danced off the tin roofs of the houses ahead of them.

'Feels good,' said Peri. 'Should be going for a swim.'

'Like where?'

'Just a thought.'

They ducked under the police tape and headed back the way they had come the day before.

'You think someone is going to have written on our photo, don't you,' said Peri.

'Maybe.' Red stared down the road ahead of her. She couldn't tell him that she had a picture in her mind, a firm picture that on that photo would be words written by her mum or her dad. They would say they were looking for her. They were so relieved to have found her. It was a miracle. They were there in the building, maybe standing right next to the photo, waiting for her to come back in to check the board. They would see her coming and they would run to her with arms outstretched. There would be tears. They were her family, they knew her name and they recognised her and she would know them.

She didn't look at the front yards where people were stacking the smashed-up garden furniture, bits of fence railing, bricks and concrete. She followed Peri, stepping around the holes in the footpath, moving aside for an old man in a wheelchair who wheezed and hissed past them.

● ● ● ● ●

It was just as the day before. Children were playing with hoops and balls on the grass while there were huge crowds of people, some heading for the building, others just standing around waiting for something to happen. There was a hum, a buzz of background noise. Red couldn't hear individual words but it was as if everyone was talking, questioning, filling the air with their voices.

They joined the queue that snaked towards the doors. Red clenched her fists so tightly that her nails dug into her palms. Pain ripped through the cuts and torn sections of skin. She forced her hands to spread open. Someone would have written on her photo. They must have. Peri was at the door first. He shouldered his way past those who were ahead of him and got to the boards. Red was through the door. The crowd drew her past the first board and then she heard Peri's voice.

'Red, Red. Quick. Look!'

She stumbled past a couple to reach him. There must be something. Her mum? Her dad? Beneath the words they had written was scrawled:

Ruby Martin? You look like my friend Ginger from Year Five.

Jazz

0464819556

And I didn't know you had a brother.

CHAPTER FIVE

JAZZ. JAZZ AND GINGER.

She is the girl sitting next to me. The broken arm. It wasn't the monkey bars, it was racing on rollerblades. Across the playground we went, holding hands, the fastest twins in the Universe. Then Jazz hit a crack in the concrete and over she went, both of us sprawled at the feet of half our class and Mr Tomkin. He went off his brain. Jazz was screaming. I was all right. The ambulance. Hospital. Plaster.

Peri was shaking her. 'What's going on? Who's this Jazz?'

'I think I remember her. She was my best friend. The girl in the photo. The one with the broken arm.'

'Let's phone her, then. She'll know who you are. Where your parents are. She can tell you why you aren't in the Year Six photo.'

Red tore the message from the bottom of the page.

Ruby Martin? You look like my friend Ginger from Year Five.

Jazz

0464819556

And I didn't know you had a brother.

She folded it over and over into a tiny square and slipped the paper into her pocket. Jazz could tell her who she was. Jazz could fill the huge empty space in her head. She could answer all the questions, tick all the boxes.

What happened after the accident? After the broken arm? Red pushed her way through the crowd, out onto the grass. Nothing. No pictures in her head of parents. No pictures of Jazz beyond the sprawling and the school photo. What had happened next?

They sat in the sunshine and broke open another packet of jellybeans. Red tossed a handful into her mouth.

'We could borrow a mobile,' said Peri, 'or nick one. You can call her and then maybe we could meet her and she can tell you everything you want to know.'

Red couldn't look at him. 'It's weird.' She tugged at a piece of grass, pressed her fingernail into the centre of the leaf and slit it neatly in two. 'Telling me won't be enough. I need to remember. I need to know it to believe it.'

'But if she tells you something, that might make you remember.'

'Maybe. It's just strange.'

'Just do it, Red.'

Was he trying to get rid of her? He'd found her and now he could hand her over to someone who knew her. His job was done. He could deliver her to Jazz. Red followed him to the room where they had had their photo taken. Peri spoke to the woman behind the desk and came back with a mobile phone. Red unfolded the paper and passed it to him.

Peri pressed the buttons, standing so close to Red that she could hear the echo of each number as it dialled. Then the ringtone. She counted the sounds. Three, four, five. Maybe Jazz didn't have her phone with her. Maybe it was lying on the floor of her room and she was outside. Maybe she'd lost her phone. Maybe...

'Hello?'

Peri pushed the phone into Red's hand.

'Hello? Who's that?'

'Um...it's Ginger.' She'd said it. It sounded like a word from another language, a word whose meaning she couldn't quite understand.

'GINGER! It *was* you in that photo. Fantastic. It's you. Muuuum! It's Ginger. This is soooo good. Soooo fantastic. But who is that boy? You don't have a brother, do you? Did you get one when…doesn't matter. Is he a boyfriend? This is so good…so cool. Where are you? When can I see you? And how come you said your name was Ruby Martin?'

'Um…I don't know. Where are you?'

'At home. Agh, you don't know this house. We moved. A year ago. Where are *you*?'

'At the place where you saw the photo. We…I was in all the mess of the storm. It's a long story.'

'Tell me when you see me. Hang on a sec.'

Red heard murmuring in the background. She put her hand over the phone and whispered to Peri, 'I think she's getting her mum to bring her over here. What'll we do?'

He shrugged. 'Go with it. Might get a decent feed. Do you remember her mum?'

Red shook her head.

'Wait at the Centre.' Jazz's voice was loud, organised. 'Be on the grass near that main door. We're coming over there and Mum's not working today and she said she'll bring you back here for the afternoon. It'll be great. I can't wait to see you.'

'Yeah.'

'See you.'

'Yeah, see you.'

They took the phone back in to the woman. 'A happy result?' She smiled a dazzling white smile and raised her eyebrows.

'Happy enough,' said Peri and they walked quickly back into the sunshine. 'How long will they be?'

'I don't know. I didn't ask.'

'When they come, might be good if I don't go with you.'

'You sure?'

'You'll have all this girl stuff to talk about. You won't want to have me hanging around.'

'Where would you go?'

'Around. I'll be OK.'

They were at the door to the Centre. Red took a deep breath. 'Peri, will you please come? I mightn't like Jazz any more. She mightn't like me. I can't remember anything about her family. I mightn't like them. They might try to boss me around and tell me what I have to do. I don't want to go by myself.'

He didn't hesitate. He shrugged. 'OK. But they'd better feed us. And it had better be good.'

• • • • •

'Ginger!' Red heard Jazz before she saw her. Then she was there. Tight black curls, arms waving, Jazz ducked and weaved her way through the crowd. She stopped. Red stared. Then suddenly they had arms around each other, cheeks pressed together, Jazz was laughing and

Red was struck dumb. She did remember. She knew this person. She really knew her. Red drew back and looked at her. Jazz too.

Then Jazz turned to Peri. 'I'm Jazz.' She held out her hand.

'Peri. And I'm not her brother but it's a long story.'

'Tell me later. Mum's got the car up the street.' She linked her arms through theirs and almost dragged them over the grass to the road.

The woman leaning against the black four-wheel-drive was a stranger. She put her arms around Red. 'So lovely to see you again after so much.' Red's nose pressed against the gold chains around her neck and breathed in a sickly perfume.

'Mmmm,' was all Red could say.

'And who is this young man?'

'This is Peri.' Red pulled back and watched as Jazz's mum held her hand out.

'Hop in the car,' she said. 'I thought I'd just take you back to our place where you can tell us what happened and you can have some lunch. We can work it out from there.'

They headed west, leaving the Centre and the coast behind them. Tree branches were down and pushed to the edge of the road. They saw a car crushed by a whole tree trunk and every now and then a house with flapping roof iron and builders working to restore it.

They drove slowly through the heavy traffic.

'The trains are all out,' said Jazz's mum. 'The underground is flooded and the electricity in these suburbs is gone. Lots of the city network is down.'

'Where are we actually going?' said Red.

'We're living in Burwood now,' said Jazz. 'It's OK there. We moved so I could go to high school. Remember how we were always going to do that together?'

Red nodded. She didn't remember that, but now wasn't the moment to say so. They drove on. Red turned her face to the window. Now there were streets full of whole houses almost untouched by the winds and the water. Pedestrians streamed along footpaths and ducked in and out of crowded shops. Cyclists in canary-coloured jackets darted between the cars. It was suddenly a different world.

●　●　●　●　●

They sat eating lunch on the wide verandah. Jazz's mum fussed around them, bringing bowls of pasta and salad and jugs of iced water. She took a camera from the bookcase inside and Red and Jazz sat together, arms around each other, posing, laughing and smiling. Then Red sucked spirally pasta into her mouth with tomato sauce, garlic, herbs and olives. It felt familiar. Was this what she was used to eating?

Peri slurped on his second helping. Red's eyes danced from the neatly mown lawn and the dense herb garden of basil and mint to the sprawling grevillea. Wattle birds balanced on the thin branches, their beaks pressed into golden flowers. Had she lived in a place like this? Did she sit eating lunch on a verandah looking out at a garden and birds? A tiny skink slid over the sandstone wall of a flowerbed.

'OK.' Jazz pushed her plate to the side and leant back from the table. 'OK. How come your photo was up on the wall? And where's your dad?'

'I don't know,' said Red. 'And how come you went to the Centre? Were you caught up in all the storm too?'

'No way. You know how Mum was a teacher. Well now she works for the Department of Education and they sent her over there with some others to work out what to do with all the kids. Schools have been wrecked, but the kids have to go somewhere. I just went with her to have a look. But I don't get it. How come you two got together?'

'Peri found me,' said Red. 'He found me lying in the mud, in the middle of all the broken-up trees and the wrecked houses and everything.'

'She was half dead,' said Peri. 'Too much eating of mud and sea-water.'

'And you don't know where your dad is?'

'I don't know anything. I can't remember anything.' Red scratched at the dry timber of the table. 'I don't know why. Maybe I got hit on the head or something. I can't picture anything; parents, the house I lived in, nothing. I couldn't remember you, Jazz, or that I was called Ginger. Not till I saw your note.'

'You mean, if I hadn't put that message up you wouldn't have known about me?'

Red shook her head.

'But we went to kindergarten together. You've known me since we were five.'

'Doesn't matter. You can say that but I can't remember it.'

'And your family? Your dad? Can you remember him?'

Red didn't answer. Her head, her whole body, felt suddenly heavy. Too many questions. Shut up, Jazz.

'So that's when you went and put that photo up?'

Peri nodded.

'But why were *you* there? Do you live round that area?'

Peri didn't answer.

Jazz wouldn't let up. 'You must have a family, Peri. Where are they?'

'I don't live with them any more.' He looked away.

'So where did you sleep last night?'

'At your old school,' he said. 'We just wanted to get away from where everything was wrecked and I thought the school was a good place, lots of rooms. It's damaged but we could get in. We slept in the library.'

Jazz laughed. 'In Mrs Mac's library. I wish I'd been there.'

'And we saw the photos on the wall,' said Peri. 'We knew then that it was Red's – Ginger's – school. Except she's not in the Year 6 photo, the one from last year.'

'That's 'cos you'd gone.' She looked at Red.

'Gone? Where did I go?'

'Good question,' Jazz shrugged. 'They came and got you from class. Your dad and another bloke. They said you had to go then, straight away. So you packed your bag and left. We thought it was something just for that day, or maybe a few days, but that was the last time we saw you. And it was terrible because you were in the class performance, you know, the one we used to do for Assembly. And when you didn't come back the next day, or the next, they had to cancel it, move it on to the next week and stupid Trevor Ho got to sing the song. You'd have been much better.'

The class performance. *I am crying in the car. But I have to sing I am saying and Dad is there and he's saying that he is sorry really sorry but this is important, more important than anything in my whole life and we are going, we have to get out of the city now, right now. My bags are packed and I can't say goodbye to anyone and we are going where the people who are after him will never find him. I am kicking the back of the seat in front and I am saying that I don't care I want to sing and he doesn't care and Mrs Williams says it is the best class performance she's ever programmed and I am the star. He turns from the front passenger seat and he hasn't shaved his face and it looks all furry. My dad is crying and he's saying he's sorry, sorry, sorry. This is not how he planned it, he thought we would never have to do this again, but we have to go to another place, to change our names and to never come back and it's to save our lives and it's for our own protection.*

Red jumped up and moved to the end of the verandah. Her shoulders were shaking. She could see his face. Dark bushy eyebrows, the deep vertical crease between them as he spoke that afternoon, a tiny scar above his lip, pale against the darker colour of his skin. And then they were at the airport and on a plane and he said they were going to Adelaide and then to a smaller place in the country and her name was different, now it was Rosie.

'What was my name?' Red turned to face Jazz. 'Not Ginger. What was my real name?'

CHAPTER SIX

'RHIANNON. RHIANNON CHALMERS. I CALLED YOU Rina. I mean when I wasn't calling you Ginger.'

Rhiannon? Chalmers? They meant nothing.

'Rhiannon, Rosie, Red, Rina, Ruby.' Peri ticked the names off on his fingers. 'Bit stuck on "R", don't you think?'

'Not my fault.' Red sat down again. 'Why did we go away? My dad said we needed protection. Who from? Why?'

'Maybe your dad was in danger from some big-time crooks. Or maybe he was a crook himself,' said Peri.

'Don't be stupid.' Red spat the words out.

'Or a spy or something like that. And he knew stuff and...'

'That sounds stupid, too,' said Jazz. 'He was just like any other dad. He took us all camping in Year Four and he made the best birthday cakes.' She looked at Red. 'Do you remember that year when we won the soccer and he made the cake like a field with green icing and...'

● ● ● ● ●

Red felt suddenly cold. Her dad, just like anyone else's dad. Her hands were tightly clasped in her lap. She whispered, 'And what about my mother?' There had been no mother in the car, at the airport, on the plane.

Jazz shook her head. 'I don't know. There never was one at your place. I don't know what happened to her. Mum might know.' She went inside then and came back with a bowl of pistachio nuts. 'I'll go and fix it with Mum so you can stay tonight.'

Red and Peri rubbed the skins off the nuts and ate in silence.

'D'you want to stay here for the night?' said Peri.

'I suppose so. I don't know what I want. But when she tells me stuff like the day we left, I do remember bits. If I stay here, more might come back. What about you?'

'I'll stay tonight. Tomorrow...' He shrugged. 'I'll work it out then.'

• • • • •

They stayed.

Jazz's mother studied Red's scabbed hands and insisted on bathing them in warm water and smoothing an antiseptic cream all over them. She found plastic gloves for Red, who then stood under the hot shower and soaped and soaped her body. She turned her face upwards and let the warm droplets pound her forehead and cheeks. Water poured over her back and her arms, taking with it the mud and salt that was in her hair and every pore of her skin. Finally she emerged. She dressed herself in Jazz's spare pyjamas and settled into an armchair in the lounge room.

'Your turn,' she said to Peri.

The television screen was filled with images of the wrecked coastline. The helicopter filming swooped low over cliffs now smashed and shattered on the beaches. Huge front-end loaders like teams of dinosaurs moved through the streets. They scooped up mud, sand and the wreckage of homes, tipping everything into the council dump-trucks. Workers in fluorescent clothing swarmed over the remains of buildings, roads and open spaces. A face appeared on the screen.

'Now here is the Prime Minister,' said the announcer.

'My government has done and will continue to do everything we can to assist everyone marked by this terrible tragedy,' said the Prime Minister. 'This is every bit as big a disaster as Cyclone Tracy that destroyed Darwin on Christmas Eve in 1974 or the Queensland cyclone and Brisbane floods of 2011. Because of the density of our current coastal urban environment, many people are now homeless. Resources are being moved in from interstate and we are grateful for the assistance coming to us from our international friends. Clearly this state of emergency will take time to resolve, but we are in this for the long haul. We are a resilient people. We will move forward. All efforts are being made by the different services to bring aid to anyone and everyone affected by what has happened.'

Numbers flashed across the bottom of the screen as she spoke: *confirmed dead 800, missing believed to be a further 650...estimated homes destroyed 10000 ...businesses, schools and other places of learning 6000...government appealing for blankets, tents...international messages of sympathy...donations of money are the best ways to help...Premier believed to be among the dead...significant destruction up and down the coast...worst-affected area the eastern suburbs of Sydney.*

• • • • •

Jazz left her seat and pushed into the space beside Red. 'This is so horrible. You don't think it can happen in your place, your country.'

Red nodded. Her eyes were fixed on the images on the screen. Was her dad one of the 800? Was he one of the 650? How could she ever find out?

Jazz slipped her arm through Red's. 'This is like when we were little and had sleepovers. Do you remember the scary movies we used to watch? And that time when we pigged out on all the lollies and you threw up on the doona that had Hannah Montana on it?'

Red didn't answer.

'While you were in the shower,' Jazz went on, 'I spoke to Mum and she says that you and Peri can stay here till we find out what happened to your dad.'

'But that might take forever.'

'So you'll stay forever. We've got room.'

'Thanks, but what'll your dad say?'

'He'll do whatever Mum and I want.'

'Where is he?'

Jazz shrugged. 'At work. He doesn't get in till really late. Since the cyclone they cancelled all the police leave. He's been taken off his usual job and is just working on this. They're all doing overtime looking for people and trying to fix stuff.'

So Jazz's mum was a teacher and her dad was a policeman. What was her own dad? How come he needed protection? How could she get from that plane trip with her dad to the mud when Peri found her? Where had she been for those two years?

• • • • •

She lay between the cool linen sheets in the extra bed in Jazz's room. Peri was down the hall in a spare room. Clearly Jazz's family had money. Had her family been like that too, with spare rooms, heavy old-fashioned furniture, fancy plates on the dinner table? As they'd eaten, Jazz's mum and dad had quizzed them about the past few days.

'Have you registered with us, with the police?' her father had said.

Peri shook his head. 'I don't need to. I'm not lost.'

'But your family, they must be worried about you. We should get in touch with them.'

'I've been in touch. They're fine and Red didn't have a name so we couldn't report her.'

Jazz's dad raised an eyebrow. 'Well at least we've solved that problem.'

Red had been silent all through the meal. Now she took a deep breath and said to Jazz's parents, 'Can you tell me something about my dad?'

'I only met him a couple of times,' said Jazz's mother. 'His name is David. And he used to drop you over to play.' She smiled at Red. 'He was very nice, a lovely man. I'm not sure where he worked or what he did.'

'Finance, I think,' said Jazz's father. 'One of those big companies. I'm not really sure exactly.'

'And my mother?'

Jazz's mum shook her head. 'I'm sorry, I don't know. I think she must have passed away. It was always just you and your father.'

Jazz's dad glanced up at the clock. 'You kids should get a good night's sleep and in the morning we'll work out what to do.'

Rhiannon Chalmers, daughter of David Chalmers who worked in some big company. Red silently said the words over and over. They were a foreign language. They belonged to a different person who came from a different world.

• • • • •

'I can't sleep. It's just so weird and so amazing that you're here.' Jazz pushed herself up on her elbow. 'What do you want to do tomorrow? We could hang out, go to a movie, that's if anything's open. Dad said the whole city is shut down. We'd have to go out to the suburbs. The trains into town aren't working. We'll have to get you some clothes, and I'll put a message up on Facebook with a photo. I'm still friends with some of the kids you'll remember from primary school. We can meet up or we could go out with my new friends, whatever.'

'I don't know.' Red stared up at the plaster rose around the light in the centre of the ceiling. Jazz didn't get it. This wasn't like before. This wasn't normal life. I don't know who I am, Red whispered to herself, and you don't understand that. You've got no idea how it feels. I'm empty. I don't belong, not here, not to you, not to anyone, not even to Peri.

'Anyway,' Jazz pushed herself out of bed and came and sat on the edge of Red's bed. 'What's that thing you're wearing around your neck?'

'This locket?'

'Yeah.'

'I don't know. It feels like the only thing I've got from before. I was wearing it when Peri found me.'

'You must have been wearing something else!'

'Yeah, sure. But that was just dirty old clothes.'

'Is there something in it? A photo?'

'Dunno. We did try to open it before but it was too hard. We didn't really have anything sharp enough.'

'I'll get something.' Jazz leapt from the bed and disappeared towards the kitchen.

She came back with a small sharp knife. Red lifted the leather cord from around her neck and laid it on the sheet. 'I should do it.' She took the knife from Jazz and tried to wedge it into the place where the two sides of the locket sealed. At first nothing happened. She twisted and turned the tip of the blade, scratching away the thin layer of mud and salt. Then the tip slipped between the two edges and slowly she drew it along the length of the locket. It sprang open and out fell a small piece of black plastic, a couple of millimetres thick. Red turned it over in her hand.

'It's a memory stick,' said Jazz. 'A USB. Quick, let's see what's on it.'

Red rolled the small object around in her palm. A memory stick. Could it have memories she didn't have? Could it tell her who she was and what had happened in the last two years? 'Give it to me.' Jazz was now sitting at her desk, her computer on. Red hesitated, then held out her hand.

After a few moments a box appeared on the screen. 'Lucky it's working,' said Jazz and she leant forward and began typing her password. First a brand name and then a long list of file names came up. She clicked on 'removable disk'. More file names. She clicked on the first one.

A face appeared.

'Dad.' Red grabbed the back of Jazz's chair. 'That's my dad,' she whispered as Jazz stood up and let her fall into the seat in her place.

• • • • •

'My name is David Chalmers and I am creating this file because I fear for my life and that of my daughter. If you are in possession of this, please deliver it to Justice John Stanton, Federal Royal Commissioner currently conducting hearings in Melbourne and Canberra. This

matter is urgent. Do not, under any circumstances, allow it to fall into the hands of any other person. Do not take it to the police. Trust no one. I repeat, no one.'

He paused then and the camera panned across a desk covered in thick piles of paper.

'I'm scanning all these documents to make a full record of my investigations into the company Jamieson Finance, done during my time as an undercover agent working with the company in Sydney. When I have finished scanning I will place the original documents in a safe place and give the details of where they can be found.

'I cannot stress too highly that there are those who will do everything possible to prevent this information from getting to the Royal Commission. Whoever you are watching this, you may be in danger, as indeed I am myself. Already some attempts have been made on my life. I repeat, trust no one. Do not take this to the police. Take great care.'

The screen went blank.

Red stared. It was the face she remembered, the one from the aeroplane, but the words were strange, unreal.

'What should we do?' whispered Jazz. She sat curled up on her bed, her arms wrapped around her knees, fingers interlaced, her knuckles white.

Red didn't answer.

'I'll get my mum or dad.'

'No.' Red shook her head. 'Get Peri.' She didn't turn her head as Jazz obediently left the room.

• • • • •

Peri said nothing as they played the video clip again.

'And that's your dad?' he said to Red as the image faded. 'Wow.'

She spun the chair round to face him. 'That's him. Not Jay Martin or James Martin. I know it's him but I can't remember much about him. I can close my eyes and I can see the day you found me. I remember that. And I remember everything that has happened since. But except for that day on the aeroplane I don't really remember him.'

'Do you know anything about what he's talking about? About people trying to bump him off?'

Red shook her head.

'Maybe the company he's investigating got a hit-man out to get him. It's like a crime movie.'

'It's real life,' said Red.

'Well, let's have a look at some of the other files.'

'No. I don't think we should. He says they're important and that's enough.'

'We have to tell Mum and Dad,' said Jazz. 'They'll know what to do.'

'He said tell no one,' said Red.

'My parents aren't no one.'

'Your dad's a policeman. He said not to tell them.'

Jazz was slumped on the bed. 'Why would he say that? This is really weird.'

'Everything's weird now,' said Red. She leant forward and closed down the file and removed the memory stick. 'We're not going to tell anyone now. In the morning we'll work out what to do.' She turned off the computer, and sealed the memory stick back in the locket. It felt cold against her chest. 'Let's go back to bed.' She didn't know what she wanted to do. She couldn't think with Jazz and Peri there. She wasn't sure she could think with them gone.

Peri looked at her and shook his head slowly. Then he turned to go.

''Night, Red.'

''Night, Peri.'

Jazz climbed slowly back into bed and said nothing.

● ● ● ● ●

Red pulled the sheet up to her neck, her father's words tumbling around in her head: *'in danger... commission...trust no one...do not take this to the police...attempts on my life'*. Why couldn't they go to the police? Isn't that what people did when they were in trouble? What did it all mean? And Peri said maybe the company had someone out to kill him. Could that be true? And where was he now? And who was Jay Martin?

Her eyes became more accustomed to the darkness and she saw pinpricks of light on the ceiling. Yellow stars of all different sizes were scattered there, as if tossed at random. Earlier, in the half light, they had been invisible. It took the darkness to uncover them.

I am lying on cool grass staring at the sky. 'That's the Milky Way,' he's saying. It's Dad. I know it's him although I can't see him. 'It's made up of well over a hundred billion stars, maybe two hundred billion or some people say four hundred billion. We're part of it and our sun is twenty-four thousand light years away from the centre.' We lie there in silence. 'They're huge but most of them have no names and we know so little about them. Makes you feel pretty small and insignificant,' he says.

CHAPTER SEVEN

RED WOKE MANY TIMES IN THE NIGHT. SHE HEARD
Jazz's even breathing and occasionally the low hum of
a car on the road. She pictured the face on the
computer screen and struggled to drag memories
from deep inside herself. Could she place him eating
breakfast across a table from her, walking beside her
on her way to school, sitting beside her in a lounge
room watching television? Nothing. She was lying
still, staring up at the ceiling stars when the alarm on
Jazz's phone rang: a song she didn't recognise.

• • • • •

'I'm going to have a shower,' said Jazz. 'Then we should tell Mum and Dad.'

Red shook her head. 'We can't tell anyone.'

'But they'll know what to do.'

'We can't. He said not to and especially not to tell a policeman.'

'Are you saying my dad's a crook or something?'

'I'm just trying to do what my dad said.'

'Dad could look your dad up on the police computers. There's sure to be stuff on there about this commission thing.'

'We can't do that.'

'Aren't you ever going to tell anyone? That's crazy.'

'I don't know. Not yet. And don't you say anything. It's my stick and my dad and he said not to tell anyone.'

'OK. OK. Don't go off at me.'

At breakfast they hardly spoke. Peri sat opposite them and looked from one to the other, raised his eyebrows, shrugged and then added another Weet-Bix to the four already in his bowl.

Jazz's mum rapped the granite benchtop with her scarlet fingernails and said, 'We want to talk to you all. Andrew and I are pretty concerned at what's happening. He's in the study. He's working at home this morning. When you finish, go and see him.' She left.

Red looked across at Jazz. 'Have you told?'

Jazz shook her head. 'When could I? You've been with me all morning.'

• • • • •

'Sit down,' Jazz's father stayed standing. Red fixed her eyes on his shoes.

'Now, Margaret and I have been talking. We are really happy to have you stay with us. Both of you are truly welcome here for as long as you like. With all the chaos outside, it may take a long time to find your families anyway, and we don't want you out there, on your own, but...' He paused.

There was a deep scratch on the outside of the shoe on his left foot. How could that have happened?

'...but we insist that we report your presence here to the authorities.'

'To the police?' said Peri.

'Well, yes. Someone may be looking for you. We need to register you so that in that case they can find out where you are.'

'But—'

'No buts, Peri. I know you said you've been in contact but given everything that's happened, if I was your dad I'd be worried sick.' He looked at Red. 'We need to find out what's happened to your father. We've made a decision. We can't do it today because I've got a conference call starting in less than an hour and then some meetings. Jazz's probably told you I'm co-ordinating the post-cyclone team and we're still in search and rescue. But first thing tomorrow morning I'll take you in to the local police station and see what paperwork we have to fill out. They might hear something or see something on all the stuff that crosses their desk and they'll make the connections. We'll need your full name, Peri.'

For a moment Red thought Peri was going to object but he swallowed hard, nodded and said, 'OK.'

Why was he agreeing?

'And you, Rhiannon, we think it's important that you are examined by a doctor. You may have had a nasty knock on the head. You could need X-rays. So we'll make an appointment to get you checked after we've been to the station.'

Red frowned but said nothing. No way. She looked across at Peri again but he had turned away from her. She didn't know what to say.

'That's settled, then. Off you go now. I've got some work to do.' He sat down at his desk and was already typing on his computer as Red, Peri and Jazz left the room.

• • • • •

'Why did you say OK?' hissed Red. They followed Jazz out onto the verandah. 'I don't want to go onto some register.'

'We won't,' said Peri. 'We can't. If your dad was right about some blokes looking for him, trying to kill him, they'll know his name and your name. If it goes on a database that someone could hack into, they'll find you. We have to get that stick to that judge wherever he is.'

'And how are we going to do that?'

Peri shrugged. 'Dunno. But I reckon that's what we have to do.'

They moved onto the grass under the wattle tree, away from the house.

'We could google the Stanton guy and find out where he is,' Jazz said.

'And then,' said Peri 'we just clear out and find him. But we've got no money, no transport. Red, your dad said he was in Canberra or Melbourne. I don't know how far away they are but it sure is too far to walk. And the trouble is that even if we got there, he wouldn't listen to us. People like him have all these security blokes around them and people like us can't get in to see them.'

'We have to try,' said Red. 'Have you got any money?' She turned to look at Jazz. 'Or could you get us some?'

Jazz nodded. 'Go and google him and I'll check it out.'

• • • • •

Nineteen thousand four hundred hits came up when they put in Justice John Stanton. Red scrolled down through articles about him, taken from newspapers and websites, lectures he had given at universities and entry after entry of pieces he'd written to comment on the law.

'What was it your dad said he was doing?' asked Peri.

'Some commission or something like that. Royal, I think.'

Entering that brought up dozens more hits. Red scanned the pages: drug lords, police corruption, money laundering, global syndicates, missing gang members, murder. She turned to Peri. 'This is unreal, like a movie. He's the boss of a big kind of investigation. Drugs and cops and stuff like that. But how would Dad fit in with all that?'

'Maybe he's a private investigator or an undercover cop and he worked for this commission. See if you can find out where it is.'

Red pointed to the screen. 'This article just went up yesterday. *Despite the dramas interstate caused by the damage in Sydney and other parts of the eastern seaboard, the Royal Commission will continue to take evidence,' Mr Justice John Stanton said today. 'Some of those who were to appear before the Commission are missing, believed to be deceased, but the Commission has many areas to pursue and our work will continue in Melbourne.'*

Red pointed to the words, *missing, believed to be deceased*. 'That might be my dad,' she said quietly. 'So, how do we get to Melbourne?'

'Google that too.'

They were scrolling through railway timetables when Jazz came back into the bedroom waving a credit card. 'We can use this. By the time Mum finds out I've taken it we'll be back and we can tell her all about it.'

'We?' Red raised her eyebrows.

'If you're going off somewhere, I want to come too.' Jazz held onto the card. 'Come on, Ginger.'

'It will be more expensive with three and it could be dangerous.'

'I've got the card,' said Jazz.

Peri shrugged. 'I reckon it's OK. She should come.'

'OK.'

Peri and Red stepped back and watched as Jazz settled herself in front of the computer. She clicked through to the train booking page. 'What names do you want me to put in?'

'Peri and Ruby Martin.' Peri pointed at Red. 'You've got more names than a whole footy team.'

Jazz typed in the details of the credit card. The completed tickets came up and she pressed Print. 'Tomorrow morning,' Jazz said, 'we get the train at Strathfield because that's the closest station where the country trains stop. Eight o'clock in the morning and we should get there about half an hour before that to find our seats.'

'How do we get there?'

'Walk. It's not far. I've done it heaps of times.'

• • • • •

In the afternoon Jazz pulled T-shirts and shorts from her chest of drawers and held them up for Red. 'You have to have a couple of spares. You can't wear the same ones all the time.'

'Peri wears the same ones all the time.'

'Boys can get away with it.' She held up a pink top with ruffles around the neck.

Red laughed. 'I don't remember much, Jazz, but I reckon I never wore stuff like that, it's not me.' She sifted through the clothes scattered on the bed. She chose a black T-shirt with swirls of muted green and red that made a spiral pattern, and a pair of black jeans. 'These'll do.'

● ● ● ● ●

'I want to leave a note for Mum and Dad,' said Jazz. 'They're going to freak out.'

It was seven o'clock. They were in her room filling their backpacks with fruit and drinks from the kitchen.

'Don't tell them where we're going,' said Red. 'They'll just follow us.'

'Tell them not to go to the police.' Peri hoisted his bag over his shoulder.

'Dad is the police,' said Jazz.

'Well, tell them Red has remembered something and we are just checking it out and we'll contact them tonight or tomorrow.'

'Like I said, they're going to freak out,' said Jazz.

'Too bad.' Red wanted to leave before Jazz backed down. There was a purpose now. This commissioner would know who her father was, maybe know what had happened to him, might even know who was after him, who wanted to kill him. Maybe getting the memory stick to the commission might save her dad's life. As she pressed the apples down into her bag, her hand brushed the book she'd taken from the school library. For a moment she thought of taking it out and leaving it on Jazz's desk. Her fingers felt the smooth, hard cover. She withdrew her hand, empty, and zipped up the pack.

Jazz scribbled a note and placed it in the middle of her pillow. As they moved quietly along the hallway they could hear Jazz's parents talking over breakfast on the back verandah. Peri opened the front door and they tiptoed through.

They didn't speak as Jazz led them along the footpath to the main shopping strip and across the park. Ahead of them was the railway line and after ten minutes they could see the sprawl of buildings that made up the station.

● ● ● ● ●

They were back in the chaos. The station was swarming with people. Adults with anxious faces clutched the hands of children who ran to keep up. A constant stream of double buses pulled up, each spewing dozens of new arrivals onto the footpaths. Salvation Army officers handed out free coffee and sandwiches. Men in uniforms with loudhailers shouted at the crowd. 'If you're heading north take platform one, south take platform four.'

'Melbourne?' said Red as she, Peri and Jazz put their hands out for sandwiches and drinks.

'South.'

She turned to Jazz as they headed towards the platform. 'Are there always this many people here?'

'No. I've never seen it like this. Must be everyone just wanting to get out and away from Sydney.'

Red nodded. Jazz's house was cool and calm but it was a world away from what was going on in the city and the destruction near the beaches. It felt weirdly good to be out in it again.

They found the right carriage and swung their bags up onto the racks over their heads.

A young woman was there ahead of them, her thin body pressed against the corner beside the window. Her eyes were red and tired-looking but she smiled at them. 'You escaping the mess too?'

'Sure are,' said Peri.

'Where are you going?' Jazz sat down next to the stranger. 'I'm Jazz and that's Peri and Red.'

'Kate. I'm off to Wagga. It's where my mum lives. I can't wait to get there. I just feel like a bit of Mum care. You know, ask no questions, just put you to bed with a hot-water bottle or a bowl of soup.'

'Were you in the big mess, then?' said Peri.

She nodded. 'Up on the Northern Beaches.' She began to cry. The tears trickling over her cheeks took with them smears of black mascara. 'My friend and I…we've lost everything…our cats, birds, garden…' She took a tissue from her pocket and blew her nose. 'Our house was knocked down. It's completely gone. In a funny way we were lucky. We were having dinner with some friends in another suburb, away from it all or at least from the worst of it. They reckon that the whole peninsula is wrecked. He's stayed down to help in the clean-up.'

'But you're both alive,' said Peri.

She nodded. 'A bit battered and bruised. And God I feel filthy.' She ran her hand through long, stringy black hair. 'What happened to you?'

'Pretty much the same. We're going to our uncle's place in Melbourne. We're all cousins and our parents are staying back to clean up, like your friend.'

While they were speaking, Red sat with her eyes pressed tightly closed. Did her mum ever tuck her into bed with a hot-water bottle and a bowl of soup? And her dad? Jazz said he made birthday cakes, special fancy ones. Did he make soup too when it was cold? She felt her stomach tighten, felt a wave of sharp, consuming fear wash over her. She jumped up and pushed her way to the end of the carriage. Her hands were trembling, then her whole body was shaking.

Why? She leant against the carriage wall. Gradually the even rhythm of the train steadied and then calmed her. She took long, slow breaths and then made her way back to her seat.

'What's up with you?' said Jazz.

'Nothing.'

● ● ● ● ●

The train was speeding its way first through red-brick suburbs and then kilometre after kilometre of high-rise apartments in slabs of dull grey concrete.

'Have you ever been out this way?' Jazz said to Peri as they reached the edge of the city.

He nodded and was about to say something when her phone rang. She took it out of her pocket and looked at the others. Both Peri and Red shook their heads. Jazz read the name on the screen. 'It's Mum,' she whispered.

'Don't answer it.' Peri leant forward and stared at Jazz, who nodded and put the phone back in her pocket.

Kate looked from one to the other and appeared to be about to say something. She closed her eyes instead and leant against the window frame.

They were in open country now, dry paddocks of grass, more yellow in colour than green. Sheep and cattle gathered tightly together in the shade of the odd gum tree. Red pressed her face against the window glass.

been fine before with just Peri. She
ve to look at him. He was sitting with
ed, looking straight ahead. What was
bout? Who was he really? Why was he
He had to have a family. Everyone had
mped in her seat. Maybe he'd had a fight
m and dad and had run away and he'd got
with the police. Or he'd been in a place
put kids who were in trouble. Hadn't he
thing about that on the first day she met

ain moved on through increasingly flat open
with occasional clumps of low bushes, a few
gum trees and fences stretching into the
. From time to time Red caught a glimpse of
bouncing off the tin roof of a farmhouse or

w much longer to Wagga?' Peri was talking to

e glanced at her phone. 'Half an hour. What are
oing to do when you get there?'
e'll be OK.'
But you want to go to Melbourne, don't you?'
He nodded. 'Are there buses?'
Yes, they go from the railway station but I don't
ow when they leave. Or you could get a ride with a
ckie. There are lots that go to Melbourne. We aren't
the freeway but they join up with it pretty quickly.'

'You look like you're dreaming,' said Jazz.

'I've got a weird feeling that I've been here before,'
said Red. 'I'm not sure though. Maybe somewhere like
this.'

'Maybe when you left with your dad.'

'Maybe...'

A beeping sound.

Jazz pulled the phone from her pocket again.
'Message,' she said, holding the phone for the others to
see.

*Where r u, ur folks keep calling me. They thnk I kno.
Txt me.*

'It's from Lisa. She's my best friend at school.'

'Text her back. Tell her we're fine.'

Jazz's thumbs danced across the pad. Red kept her
face against the glass.

• • • • •

The sun rose higher and higher. Jazz kept texting. Red
drifted into sleep.

She was woken up by a cry from Jazz. 'My God. It's
from Mum. She knows we're on the train.'

'What?' Peri grabbed the phone from her. 'Speak to
her and tell her we're OK.'

Then the phone rang. On the second ring Jazz
pressed the button to take the call. 'Yes, it's me. We're
fine. We know what we're doing.' There was a long
pause. 'No. They can't do that. No.' Jazz was shaking

her head. 'Please, Mum. You have to stop them. It's important. I don't care if he's made his mind up.' Another pause. 'I can't tell you…yes, I know, I love you too.' She hung up.

'What was all that about?' said Peri.

'God, you're not going to believe this. They know we're on the train. Dad got into my computer, don't ask me how. They found the stuff about the tickets and they just worked it out. He's talked to his mates and Mum says that they are going to be at the station at Albury and take us off.'

'They can't.' Red was sitting forward, hands clenched.

'Don't worry,' Peri said. 'The cops are too busy with all the people who are missing and the looters and everything like that. They won't worry about us.'

Jazz shook her head. 'No, you're wrong. You don't realise. Dad's really senior now. He's got mates in all kinds of places, guys he's worked with. He can just boss them around, tell them what to do. He'll have put our names in those databases already. You can bet on that. When we stop at Albury there'll be the local cops on the platform and that will be that. He could even be there himself. We'll have to tell them why we want to go to Melbourne. I should call Mum back.'

'No. There's another way.' Red spoke quietly. 'When the train gets to Albury, we won't be on it. We'll

get off whe
towards Kate

'And then
pants?' said Jaz
'We'll work t
She settled back
like this in front
was. Trust no one.

Kate was starin
stickybeak but are
something?'

Jazz shook her head
we have to get to Melbo
got—'

'Shhh,' Red frowned at
Kate screwed up her fa
danger?'

'No,' said Red. 'Well, may
plicated and dangerous and we
You can't tell anyone.' She glare

'You *mustn't* tell anyone,' she
come and ask if you've seen us,
thing, please, especially what she

The train pulled into Goulburn
'Maybe we should get out here.
face to the window.

'No. We're getting out at Wagga.'
close and her head drop forward.

come? It had
opened one e
his arms fold
he thinking
on his own?
that. She sl
with his mu
into troubl
where the
said some
him?
The t
country
straggly
distance
sunligh
shed.
'Ho
Kate.
S
you g
'

kn
tr
o

Peri nodded again.

'I should give you my mum's number,' said Kate. 'Then if you get into any hassles you could ring us and we might be able to help.'

'Thanks, but we'll be all right.'

• • • • •

The train pulled into the station at Wagga. As they stood up and dragged their bags from overhead, Kate scribbled something on a piece of paper and pressed it into Red's hand.

'You never know,' she whispered.

Crowds swarmed over the platform. People were calling out names, waving their arms and seizing those who came off the train. Kate disappeared, engulfed by a huge woman, her thick grey hair tamed into a plait that hung below her shoulders.

Red couldn't take her eyes off them.

'Come on,' hissed Peri. He grabbed her arm and they moved with the crowd slowly towards the station exit.

They stood for a moment watching people climbing into cars and taking off in all directions. Peri headed off along the wide footpath.

'Where are we going?' Jazz called.

'To find somewhere we can sit and work out what to do,' said Peri.

Red said nothing.

After ten minutes they reached a park. In the centre was an oval with cricket nets and there was a team of kids practising their bowling. Peri crossed the grass to a band rotunda and they tossed their bags down and fell onto the wooden seats.

'I don't think this was such a good idea,' said Jazz. She felt into the pocket of her backpack and took out the last of her sandwiches. 'I mean, we could be stuck here for ages with just the odd bottle of water and a stale sandwich to stop us starving to death.'

'Quit whingeing.' Peri was feeling in his own pockets. 'We just need to think of ways to get to Melbourne. What did that woman Kate say – there are buses that go there.'

'We've got no money.'

'What about your mum's credit card?'

'She probably stopped that after we got the train tickets.'

Red sat with her feet up on the seat, her chin resting on her knees. She felt the cool metal of the locket against her chest even as her face felt warm in the sun.

'Pity we can't just email all that stuff to the judge,' said Jazz. 'Then we could go home.'

'I want to give it to him myself,' said Red. 'And I have to ask him about my father.' Didn't Jazz care that there were people who wanted to kill him? That maybe the information on the USB stick might save him? That the judge would know who she was? She had to get to Melbourne.

She shook her head, stood up and leant against the upright pole at the entrance to the rotunda.

Jazz was chewing the last of her sandwich. 'We will need more stuff to eat. And drink.'

'Shut up. Food's the least of our worries. We can always nick food. It's getting to Melbourne we need to think about,' said Peri.

Jazz drew back from him. She turned and looked out through the bars of the building. 'Look, there's a police car. Maybe it's looking for us.'

'God.' Peri dropped to the floor of the rotunda. 'Your father's probably got the cops all over the state out after us.'

Red joined him.

'What will they do if they pick us up?'

'Nothing much. They'll just send us back to Jazz's place.'

'But if they know who I am … if they know about my dad and if they are the ones he was warning us about, on the USB…?'

'You don't want to think about that.' Peri waited a few moments and then lifted his head. 'No, they've gone now.' He stood up and pulled Red to her feet.

'If you two are hungry,' he said, 'we need to work out what we're going to do. We can find some shops or restaurants where they chuck out food. There's always plenty in the skips in the back lanes.'

'Yuck,' said Jazz. 'I'm not eating stuff someone's thrown away.'

'Suit yourself. Then we go back to the station where the buses go from, or a service station or wherever it is that the trucks go from and we see if anyone will take us through.'

'And if no one will?' Jazz was standing in front of him now, hands on her hips, challenging him.

'Jazz,' he said slowly, 'if you want to call your parents and go home, fine. Just give us time to get away first.'

'No, no I don't want to do that.' She was crumbling, 'I just don't want to be hungry, that's all. And I don't like the way you act as if my dad's some kind of crook.'

All this time, Red hadn't spoken. She looked from one to the other. 'If you two don't quit arguing I'm going to go off on my own.'

'OK. OK. We need to stick together,' said Peri.

'We've got no money,' said Red. 'If Kate was right, if there are trucks that go to Melbourne overnight we should try to find one. Ask some driver if he'll take us.'

'That's pretty dangerous,' said Jazz. 'A truck driver might attack us or something. My dad says people who hitch-hike are just asking for it.'

'Maybe, but what choice do we have?' Red moved over to the seats and picked up her bag. 'Anyway, no truckie's going to attack three at once. Let's go back to the station and try and find out where they go from.'

• • • • •

Peri was a few metres ahead of them. He stopped after three blocks and pointed to his right. 'There are shops down there. Why don't we see if we can get some food?' They crossed the road and soon were in a strip with restaurants, delis and shops selling fruit and vegetables. 'This is what we want.' Peri led them down an alleyway till they were in a lane that ran behind the shops. He passed his bag to Red. 'Wait here.'

She and Jazz stopped. They watched Peri pull himself up onto the edge of a huge metal skip. He hovered there for a moment, then turned, grinned and gave them a thumbs-up signal before disappearing into the bin.

For a few moments nothing happened. Then his face appeared at the top of the bin and he passed out a loaf of sandwich bread. 'It's a day or so old, but it's not green.'

Jazz screwed up her nose but reached to take it from him. A plastic bag with fruit came over next. 'There's more here, too.' Peri disappeared.

The thud of boots sounded from the far end of the lane. Three boys, their heads shaven, their T-shirts torn, came racing towards them. 'Git, you lot.' They kicked at the bin then grabbed the edge and began to shake it.

'Git. This is our patch. Git out, you in there. Git out before we smack your head in.'

CHAPTER EIGHT

JAZZ GRABBED RED'S ARM. THE METAL BIN SCRAPED
on the rough tarred surface of the road. Peri's face
appeared. The biggest of the boys screamed at him,
kicking hard with his heavy boots and then launching
himself forward.

Peri disappeared, as the boy landed heavily inside.
Screams. Thuds. Bodies smacked into the bin's sides.
More screams. The other two boys kept rocking the
bin, violently, one edge mounting the footpath, the
whole thing looking as if it might tip over.

'Stop it! Stop it!' Red launched herself at the boys.
She tugged at their shirts. 'Leave him alone! He's not
hurting you.'

'Piss off.' She was shoved roughly away.

She landed heavily on her back on the road. She pushed herself up. The bitumen tore at the scabs on her hands.

'What can we do?' Jazz was beside her, almost crying.

Red's heart was pounding in her chest. 'I don't know. I don't know.'

An upstairs window of the shop opened and a man leant out. 'Get lost, you lot. Cut the noise.'

'Cut it yourself, Grandpa,' yelled one of the boys rocking the bin.

Police sirens sounded. A van swung into the lane.

'Run.' Red grabbed Jazz's hand and ran. She ducked into an open gateway. Jazz followed. Footsteps raced past them. The girls crouched against the paling fence. The van had stopped. Two policemen stepped out. They were huge, their hips covered with a gun holster, a long, heavy baton and a radio with an aerial poking from it. They leaned over the edge of the bin, and Peri and the other boy climbed slowly out.

'Is he OK?' whispered Jazz.

'I can't tell.'

Peri's back was to them. His torn shirt hung in strips off his shoulders. A policeman stood tall over him. Red strained to hear what was being said but they were too far away. One of the policemen opened the rear door of the van. Peri and the other boy stepped around the vehicle and, as he did so, Peri turned and looked up the lane towards Jazz and Red. His face was streaked with blood.

• • • • •

Red watched as the van disappeared. She and Jazz came out of their hiding place into the empty lane.

'What do we do now?' whispered Jazz.

Red shook her head and began walking after the van.

'We can't go on without him,' said Red. She stopped in front of a waiter spreading cloths over his outdoor tables. 'Excuse me, can you tell us where the police station is?'

He waved his arm. 'This street, three blocks down.'

'Are we going to the police?' said Jazz.

'I don't know but we need to know where they've taken Peri. They might just let him go.' Red wanted to believe that. Her dad had said not to go to the police. *Trust no one. I repeat, no one.* Peri reckoned Jazz's dad would have put their names in databases for anyone to check. At least they didn't have photos. She stopped. There was a photo. Jazz's mum had taken that one at lunch. Red and Jazz on the verandah. That could be all over the country now.

They kept walking.

The rich tomato and herb smell of pizza rushed at them from the open door of the next restaurant. Then came Indian curry and Vietnamese and Thai spices. They breathed deeply, looked at each other but said nothing.

After five minutes they stood across the road from the police station. They were on a block of open ground where seats were scattered between flowerbeds and under tall trees. Jazz tossed her bag onto a seat and flopped down. 'This is hopeless. What are we going to do, Ginger?'

'I don't know.' Red sat down. After a few minutes she said, 'I keep having this weird thought. When we were little, did we have a story or a book about a kid who's really sad when her dad dies and she puts her heart in a bottle and hangs it around her neck?'

'I don't remember that,' said Jazz. 'You're right, it's really weird.'

'I remember it, though. I can see this picture of a girl wearing this bottle. It's happening to me. It's like I've got nothing inside me. It's empty. Everything's on the outside or it's gone. Like that kid. My brain is too. I can't think. I can't do anything.'

'Are you all right?'

'No.'

• • • • •

So they sat for a long time. The sky darkened. People came and went up the steps that led to the police station. Workers streamed out of the office blocks and headed for home. Red felt her emptiness overwhelming her. Shall I fade to nothing? Shall I just shrink and disappear? Be nothing? Nowhere? I have to do something. She stood up and began to pace the length of the block. One hundred and fifty steps. She turned and counted back. Her father said not to go to the police. Maybe police in a country town were different? Could she trust them? Did she have to stay away from them as well as anyone who might want to do harm, who might want what she had? She put her hand to her chest and pressed the locket against her skin. She walked the length of the block again. Peri was in there. She couldn't just leave him. She stood in front of Jazz and said, 'We need to find out what's happening. We can't stay here all night. If they are going to keep Peri in there till the morning we should go somewhere else to sleep. But if he's going to come out tonight we should wait for him.'

'Are you going to go and ask?'

'We're both going.'

● ● ● ● ●

They stood at the desk and waited. A man looked up from his computer. 'Be with you in a sec.'

They studied the faces of missing persons, girls like them pasted on the wall above a row of plastic seats. Black flyspots dotted some and others had edges that had come loose and were curling inwards. 'Least we aren't there,' whispered Jazz.

'Not yet,' said Red.

When the man came to them, Red took a deep breath and put on the most serious face she could. 'I...we are checking about our cousin. He was in a fight earlier and a police van picked him up with this other boy and we want to know when he's going to come out.'

'OK. Name?'

Whose name did he mean? What name would Peri have given?

'Your name, young lady?'

What name should she give? It would go into his computer. Onto a database.

'Rose.'

'Rose who?'

She glanced at the faces of the missing. A woman, Mitsy Walker, with long blonde hair swept across her face and rings piercing her nose, lips and eyebrows stared out at her.

'Rose Walker.'

'And where do you live, Rose?'

'We're from Sydney. Our house got destroyed in the cyclone. Our parents are still there working on the clean-up and they've sent us to friends of theirs who live down here. I can give you their name and phone number.' She pulled Kate's scrap of paper from her pocket. 'It's Mrs Michaels and the number is 696 4001.'

'Hang on a minute.' He left through a door at the back of the room.

'How did you get that?' Jazz looked at Red, wide-eyed.

'Kate gave it to me on the train. If they let Peri out, maybe we should ring Kate and sleep there. Or she might tell us where the truck place is.'

The minutes ticked by. A phone rang and went unanswered. Red slumped onto one of the plastic seats. The hard frame dug into her back and the underside of her legs. A different policeman, huge and fatherly-looking, came through a rear door and noticed Red and Jazz. 'You two young ladies need any help?'

'We're OK,' said Jazz. 'Another man is looking after us.'

More minutes ticked by.

Finally the first policeman came back, not through the door that he'd left by but through another door on the same side of the counter as Red and Jazz. With him was Peri. His face was washed, one arm was bandaged and he had on a different T-shirt.

'OK,' said the policeman. 'I should probably lock this young fella up for the night. I'm not happy with you city kids hanging out in the streets round here, but if Mrs Michaels will come and pick you up, and if she'll guarantee to keep you out of trouble, then you can go without any charge.' He waved to a phone on the wall at the end of the counter. Red took the scrap of paper and dialled the number. How could she speak so the man didn't hear?

As the dial tone rang she watched him go back to the other side of the desk and sit at his computer.

'Hello?'

'Hello, is that Kate?'

'Yes.'

'It's Red.'

'Red? From the train?'

'Yes.'

'Where are you? Are you all right? What's happened?'

'It's a long story. We've ended up in a bit of trouble and we're at the police station and they want your mum to come and pick us up.'

'My mum? Why her? OK. Hang on…'

Red heard muffled words in the background.

'OK. I'm going to come in and get you. I'll be about fifteen minutes.'

'Thanks. And Kate, I'm really sorry.'

The policeman left them then to wait.

They settled on one of the seats as far from the desk as possible.

'What was that all about?' Peri spoke as softly as he could.

Red explained. 'And I thought they were going to ask me your name and I didn't know what you'd said that was.'

He grinned at her. 'I told them my name was Dominic. Dominic Walker. I got that bit from that woman on the poster.'

Red and Jazz burst out laughing.

'What's so funny?'

'She did the same,' said Jazz. 'She's Rose Walker!'

'I knew we were related,' said Peri.

• • • • •

Kate arrived and went straight to the desk.

'You happy to look after this lot?' The policeman came towards her. 'Hey, don't I know you from somewhere? School? Back around 2000?'

Kate nodded.

'Thought I recognised the name.'

'Well, I'd better take these kids home and get them fed. See you.'

'Yeah. See you.'

They followed her out to a four-wheel drive parked under the trees.

'I'm so glad you gave me that number,' said Red.

''S all right. I thought you might need me.'

• • • • •

They drove through the empty streets past tidy houses lit only by the flickering light of television.

'Is your mum OK about this?' said Peri.

'She's a bit confused. We're both a bit confused. I told her I met you on the train and you were running from all the chaos in Sydney and she said you were welcome to a feed and a warm bed and then some help to get where you're going. Your uncle's, wasn't it? In Melbourne?'

'That's right.'

'But what happened to you, Peri? You look like you've been in a brawl.'

'Something like that.'

'It's complicated,' said Red. 'Can we explain when we get to your place?'

• • • • •

They turned into a driveway where two sprawling scarlet bottlebrushes hid the house from view. Kate drove around into the back yard. A lazy dog tied up at its kennel watched them walk up to the door.

'Come on in,' said Kate. She dropped her bag onto the kitchen bench and tossed her keys into a bowl. 'We won't bite.'

• • • • •

They sat around the large wooden table in the middle of the kitchen. Kate's mother, Anna, her long grey hair now falling loosely over her shoulders, carved a roasted chicken and dished up plates full of potatoes, carrots and peas. 'All from the garden,' she said, 'the chook included.'

Red scooped a forkful of peas and gravy into her mouth. 'Tastes great,' she said.

'So you were all in the thick of it, the cyclone I mean.'

Red nodded.

'Terrible business. It's going to take years to rebuild, that's if they do rebuild those suburbs. Some people are saying it could all happen again and they should get used to it. Imagine that, cyclones like you get in the tropics. Maybe they should turn the coastal strips into parks or something like that.'

Red took a long sip of water. Suddenly she was remembering: mud and sand in her mouth in her nose in her hair, the stinking smell of the dog carcass, the weeping, weeping people filling the Centre. Her hands shook. Peas fell to the plate, to the table, to the floor.

'Sorry,' she said. 'I just …' Her throat tightened. She pushed her chair back from the table.

Everyone was looking at her.

'Toilet's down the hall,' said Kate.

Red found the bathroom and closed the door behind her. She turned the cold tap on and splashed her face over and over again. Tears and cold water ran down her cheeks. Finally she turned the tap off, wrapped her face in a towel and sat on the edge of the bath. Her body steadied. Her breathing became normal. She looped the towel over the rack and walked back into the hallway.

Kate was standing outside the kitchen.

'Are you all right?' she said.

Red nodded.

'I get flashbacks,' said Kate, 'times when I think I'm back in the middle of it. And I didn't have nearly as bad a time as you.' She put her arm across Red's shoulder and they went back into the kitchen.

Peri was talking to Kate's mother. 'Kate said you used to be on a farm.'

'Yes. We moved into town when Kate's dad died.'

'What kind of place was it? Stock or crops?'

'Both. Cattle mainly, and wheat.'

'Did you have any horses?'

'When Kate was a kid. Why? Sounds like you're interested in farming. Is that where you live?'

'When I was a little fella. We were on a farm for a while. I used to have my own horse.'

Red watched him as he spoke. He'd dropped his voice and was stirring the gravy on his plate. What had he told her before? That his mother had died. Was that why they left the farm?

'I wish I lived on a farm.' Jazz grinned at Kate and her mother. 'It must be just so much fun.'

'More like hard work and little money,' said Kate.

'It's all right.' Anna scooped up the plates and moved them over to the bench. 'Grab some fruit and let's go into the other room. I've got some things I want to ask you people.'

She led them along the hallway and into a room filled with heavy green leather armchairs. There were dark wooden cupboards along one wall. Behind the glass doors of one were rows of old hardback books and behind another delicate teacups and plates decorated in blue and white patterns. In an alcove beside the fireplace was a wall of photographs: individuals in beautiful clothes, couples on their wedding day, children playing on the front verandah. In the centre was a large formal photograph of what looked like a whole family. Red stared at the old-fashioned clothing: long dresses on the women, high collars and dark jackets on the men. There were little children in the front row all in the same style of white pinafore.

'My great-great-grandmother,' Kate pointed to the old woman in the centre of the photo. 'She had eleven children.' She traced her finger over the straight-backed men and women. 'And this little kid here,' she touched on the smallest of the children, 'is my grandmother.'

'You are so lucky.' Red stayed in front of the photo for a long time.

• • • • •

'OK.' Kate's mother drew a deep breath. 'I'm happy to feed you kids and give you a bed for the night. I believe in the kindness of strangers and if you were mine I'd hope someone out there was looking out for you.' She paused. 'But I reckon you owe me a bit of an explanation and Kate says she got the impression you might be in some kind of danger.'

'No. No way.' Jazz smiled brightly. 'We've been in the big mess in Sydney and we're on our way to Melbourne to stay with an uncle.'

Red rolled her eyes. She looked across at Peri. He nodded.

'It's not really like that,' she said. 'We could be in danger, real danger. We just don't know. I'll tell you from the beginning.' And so she began with the moment she woke up in the mud muttering someone's name and saw Peri watching her from his position on the table. She summarised the night in the school, the discovery of her photo by Jazz and their subsequent meeting. It felt good to talk. It really was like a weight being lifted from her shoulders. She only hesitated when she got to the moment of placing the memory stick in the computer. She took a deep breath. 'It was my father. I knew it was him even though I can't really remember being with him or where we were. And the things he said are really scary. He wants us to take this stick and the files on it to this judge who's in Melbourne, in some commission.'

'That'd be the Royal Commission,' said Kate. Her mother nodded.

'And he was really heavy about not going to the police. He said it was really, really dangerous.'

'What is this commission thing?' said Jazz.

'It's an inquiry into all kinds of criminal stuff,' said Kate. 'Drugs, murder, corrupt police. They started doing the research a few years ago and maybe your dad, Red, was involved in that. The rumour is that there are quite a few police who'll lose their jobs over it. There are a couple of big-name companies involved too – companies that people think are respectable but have made millions and millions of dollars with drug-running and other criminal stuff... murder, you name it. There's a lot at stake here.'

'So anyway, we have to get to Melbourne,' said Red. 'And we got off the train because Jazz's dad had worked out where we were.'

Kate's mother had been sitting across from Red, her hands clasped in her lap. 'Slow down a minute. Why didn't you tell all this to Jazz's parents in the first place? They might have helped.'

'That's what I reckon,' said Jazz.

'I didn't want to tell anyone. My dad on the memory stick said not to tell anyone, especially not the police. Jazz's dad is in the police. I'm not saying Jazz's dad is bad, I just feel I have to do what Dad said.'

'Well,' Anna shook her head, 'you should be careful what you say. Not all police are corrupt. The majority are there to uphold the law and I'm sure they would help you get to the Commission. Some of the ones here are men I've known most of my life. They come from good families. I'm sure they aren't involved in anything that's criminal. You wouldn't be putting yourselves in any danger if you told them.'

'But we can't be sure about anyone or anything.' Red held her gaze. She was getting a bad feeling about Kate's mum – what if she decided to phone the police first thing in the morning? Then they'd be at the door and they'd call Jazz's parents and that would be that. The memory stick would be in Jazz's dad's hands, and she, Red, would be stuck. No dad...no memory...nothing.

'I don't like the idea of you just heading off to Melbourne by yourselves. You are children. This is not some game you're playing. Anything could happen to you and I'd feel responsible. In the morning we'll sort it out properly.'

'Why don't we sleep on it?' Kate stepped in. 'I'm stuffed and I'm sure you kids are.'

● ● ● ● ●

Later they lay on spare camping mattresses on the floor of the television room. Red couldn't sleep. 'I don't think they'll help us. Kate might, but not her mum.'

'You're right. She's a bit of a dragon. I reckon she's on the phone right now, dobbing us in to some mate who's a policeman. Everyone knows everyone in a town like this. We have to help ourselves,' said Peri.

'But what can we do?' said Jazz. 'This was kind of fun at the start, but not now. We should've told Mum and Dad in the first place. Then we wouldn't be in this mess.' She rolled over, turning away from the other two.

Peri moved closer to Red and whispered, 'I reckon we should get on a bus tomorrow and go on to Melbourne. We should sneak out really early and do it just the way we did for the train.'

'But we haven't got any money.'

'I've thought of that. Kate's bag is on the bench in the kitchen.'

'We can't take that.'

'Have you got a better idea? We can leave a note, tell her that we'll pay her back.'

'But we can't. You aren't listening. I said we haven't got any money.'

'If what's on that stick is as important as your dad made out, then someone is going to reward you. They'll look after you, and the cost of a bus ride to Melbourne is not much. Kate said she was here to recover a bit – she's not planning to go anywhere. She won't need money. Anyway, people like her can just go to the bank and get more. She won't miss it.'

'You don't really know that.' Red felt herself wavering. She was like a fish on the end of a line.

Peri the fisherman tried again. 'In two days, or maybe even tomorrow, you could hand over that stick.

People might know more about your dad. They might even know why you were in Sydney, where he was, everything you need to find out. But if Kate's mother has her way we'll be down at the police station telling our story to those blokes who dragged me in. They'll be dead suspicious. They'll be onto Jazz's dad quick as a flash and our names will be in databases all over the country – if they aren't already. Your dad said there are people who'll do anything to stop that stuff getting to the Commission. We don't know if it's the business people Kate mentioned, or some hitman of theirs, or if it's crooked cops or whatever, but you can bet that they'll be straight onto it. Big-time crooks hack into databases all the time. They know what's going on. They could figure out who you are and that you're on your way to Melbourne and they'll just know that it's got something to do with your dad's evidence. They'll know that they can't take the risk on you getting there.'

The fish was out of the water and on the bank. Red was nodding. 'We don't have much choice. Why don't we get a bit of sleep and then leave before it gets light.'

Peri shook his head. 'If we fall asleep we won't wake up in time. We have to stay awake and when it starts to get light, we take off.'

CHAPTER NINE

'THIS ISN'T GOING TO WORK. I CAN HARDLY KEEP MY eyes open.' Red rolled onto her side and looked across at Peri.

He was lying on his back, staring at the ceiling.

'Maybe I should tell you another story, like I did at the school. "The Three Bears", or "Three Billy Goats Gruff".'

'That's for little kids.'

'If you don't like it, you tell me one.'

'I don't know any.'

'Make something up. Or tell me a true one.'

'Like what?'

Red took a deep breath. 'Well, it's not fair. You know as much about me as I know myself. I tell you everything that I remember. I don't keep anything a secret. But I don't know anything about you. Not really. Where is your family? Why don't you live with them? What happened?'

The steady rhythm of Jazz's breathing hung in the silent room. Would he tell her something? Anything?

'It's complicated. I don't tell anyone.'

'You said at dinnertime that you lived on a farm. Tell me about that.'

'Not much to tell.' He was whispering. 'It was up till I was about ten. It wasn't a big place, not like round here. Dad managed it for some other bloke.'

'And that's when you had your own horse.'

'Yeah.'

'And why did you leave?'

'It's a long story.' Peri lifted himself up onto his elbow. 'The farm wasn't making any money. It was in the drought years and...'

Red waited.

Peri dropped back, his hands tucked under his head. He wouldn't look at her.

'...and then Mum died.'

'That's terrible. I'm sorry.'

'There was an accident. She was driving and we never knew what happened, not really, but the car ended up rolling and it was in a kind of gully and it wasn't found for hours and hours. She was dead and so was Kelly.'

'Who was Kelly?'

'My sister.'

Red wanted to reach out and touch him, to say something. She lay still and silent.

'Was she younger than you?'

'She was little, only two. And that's when we moved into town, Dad and me. We came up to Sydney to stay with my auntie for a while. That was good. She hasn't got any kids and she really spoiled me a bit. But it didn't last long 'cos she and Dad had a big fight about him drinking too much and then he got a girlfriend and Auntie May didn't like her much, even though she was the one who introduced them at the club. So we got our own place after that.'

He was quiet for a bit. Red felt wide awake. Would he go on? Would he say why he had left?

'It was all right for a while, sort of. And then she moved in with us, the girlfriend I mean.'

'Didn't you like her?'

'I hated her. They were always clearing out to the club or off with her friends. Dad and I used to do stuff before. When she came, no way.' He paused, 'I couldn't hack it. In the end I just took off.'

'Where did you go?'

'Just around.'

'But you have to sleep somewhere. You have to find food to eat.'

Peri chuckled.

'Did you steal things?'

'There's always a way. You can find places that'll feed you and there are places where you can get a bed.'

'Like the palace.'

'No. Before everything got wrecked. Before the cyclone. Churches and stuff. People on the street tell you. They can be real friendly and they look out for you.'

'But didn't you miss your dad? Didn't he come looking for you?'

'At first. A couple of times I got picked up by the cops. Once when they took me home he was there and so was she. He was all right but she just yelled and yelled at me. She said I'd done all this stuff that I hadn't done. She reckoned I should be put in a special place for bad kids and he just sat there and let her say all that. I wasn't going to stay there. No way. I took off again.'

'Don't you miss him?'

'Kind of. I miss Mum more.'

They lay silent again. What's he thinking? Is he glad he told me? I'm glad I know. Should I say something?

• • • • •

Peri was nudging her. 'Wake up, Red. We have to go.'

Tiny slivers of golden light slid through the vertical blinds. Jazz stirred. 'What's going on? Why are you…'

'Shh. We're leaving.'

Jazz pushed herself up on her elbows. 'What are you talking about?'

'We're going to leave,' said Peri. 'Red and I reckon we should get a bus this morning. If we wait, Kate's mum will dob us in.'

'We have to go, Jazz,' said Red. 'The sooner we get to Melbourne, the sooner we can go back to Sydney and life can be normal again.' She took the notebook that Peri had passed her and scribbled.

Kate,
Sorry to leave this way and for taking your money
but we have to get to Melbourne and the
Commission as soon as we can. Please, please don't
tell anyone where we've gone. We will definitely pay
you back.
Red

She tore the page from the book and left it on the pillow.

She glanced at that last sentence. How would she ever pay anyone back?

• • • • •

The street was quiet.

'Do you know where we're going?' hissed Jazz.

'Back to the railway station. That's where the buses go from.'

'It's still night-time. You're crazy.'

'Shove it, Jazz,' said Peri. 'We've just nicked money from someone. We think there might be police after us – or at least there will be by late this morning. Our plan is to get on a bus and get out of here. If you want to go home, fine. Go.'

'You're always picking on me.' Jazz looked to Red for support. She shook her head. Melbourne, that was all she could think of. If Peri and Jazz wanted to argue, that was their business.

The faint light between the trees grew deeper. All was quiet, then suddenly screeching, raucous white cockatoos swept low over them. Other birds joined in a chorus that marked the sun's rising. They saw their first cars and then a truck moving slowly along the street.

'I don't like this,' whispered Red. 'What if one of those cars is the police and they're looking for us?'

'Don't be stupid. We'll be at the station in a few minutes.' Peri quickened his pace. 'We can check the bus timetable and then if we have long to wait we'll just go down to the river or somewhere where no one can see us for a while.'

They turned a corner. The lights of the station were ahead of them. As they came towards a small shop, the truck that had been moving slowly stopped and a figure jumped out and tossed a couple of piles of papers on the step. The truck revved its engine and sped away.

Red reached down and grabbed a paper from the top of each pile. The first one was only a couple of pages and the banner headline read *Your Local News*. She glanced at the photo that almost filled the front page.

She stopped. She and Jazz were grinning, staring out from the verandah back in Burwood, their arms around each other. The headline:

Three Teenagers Missing: Parents' Desperate Search

Sydney Police Inspector Andrew Lucas and his wife Margaret are in a desperate search for their only daughter Jazz. She is believed to be travelling with two other young people, Rhiannon Chalmers and a young male who has not been identified. Police believe that Rhiannon Chalmers is suffering from a severe mental condition brought on by the loss of her family in the cyclone that devastated parts of Sydney last week. The young man is known to the police. The trio was last seen on the Sydney to Melbourne train yesterday. It is believed that they left the train in Goulburn, Junee or Wagga. They may still be in the area. Anyone seeing these young people is urged to contact their local police as soon as possible. A reward has been offered.

• • • • •

'They've got our names. We have to split up.' Red waved the paper at the others. 'It'll be in the city papers and on TV.' She was almost crying now. 'Someone could connect me to Dad, to Melbourne and the Commission. Some crooks...and everyone else will be looking for us. They'll want that reward.'

'Hang on,' said Peri. 'Calm down. Hardly anyone here will have read their paper yet. Let's get to the bus station and check the timetable. Maybe we will have to split but let's check out that bit first.'

• • • • •

At the station a woman was sweeping leaves from around the entrance and a man lounged on a seat under the window. Newspapers were piled on the footpath.

'You go and look,' said Red. 'Jazz and I'll stay back.' They sat on the grass behind a clump of oleander bushes and watched as Peri studied the timetable posted just outside the door. They saw him run his finger down a column then place his hands in his back pockets and rock backwards and forwards. Lights had come on inside the building and Peri went in.

He joined them fifteen minutes later and held a piece of paper out to Red.

'You're in luck. A ticket for you for today and the twenty bucks change. I've kept enough for Jazz and me, for later. I reckon you're right, we have to split up. You should go first and then we'll come on another bus, late this afternoon or worst case, tomorrow. Your bus will be here in about an hour. You should wait for us at the bus station in Melbourne. If something happens and we aren't on the next bus, you'll have to find the Commission yourself.'

Red glanced at the ticket in her hand. 'This says I'm sixteen. I'm not, at least, I don't think I am.'

'You are today.' Peri grinned. 'Otherwise you need all these forms with your parents' permission. And your name is still Rose Walker.'

Red looked from Peri to Jazz. 'Thanks, you two. Be careful. Kate's mum must be up now and she'll know we're gone. This is where they'll come looking.'

'We'll go down near the river,' said Peri. 'You should stay out of sight till just before the bus goes.' He waited while Jazz stepped out onto the footpath ahead of him. He turned to Red and brushed her shoulder with his hand. 'You'll be all right.'

She nodded. 'You too.'

● ● ● ● ●

Red watched as more people arrived at the station. Cars and utes pulled up and men, women and children spilled out. Gathering up their bags, they crowded into the waiting room of the station. Then a huge silver coach with red and green kangaroos painted along its side came slowly through a gate beyond the station and parked less than fifty metres from Red. People pushed forward. Red scanned the crowd for Kate and her mother. They must be up by now. They must have realised that this is where she, Peri and Jazz would go. She felt alone, exposed, even though the huge shrubs hid her from view.

A four-wheel drive swept up to the station and screeched to a stop. Kate, her hair loose over her face and dressed in a long T-shirt and jeans, jumped from the driver's seat and ran into the waiting room. In a few minutes she was back. She pressed her face to the passenger window. 'They aren't here. No one has seen them.' She put her hand up to shield her eyes from the sun and stared down the street.

Red held her breath. Part of her wanted to leap out, to tell Kate not to worry, they were fine and they would get to Melbourne and they would pay the money back. She clutched her ticket, willing Kate to get back into her car and leave. Half an hour must have passed since Peri and Jazz left. The people would soon be getting on the bus. 'Leave,' she whispered under her breath. 'Leave, leave, leave.'

Kate kept talking to her mother. Finally she moved to the driver's door, got in and the vehicle sped off.

Red counted slowly to fifty and stood up. She hitched her backpack over her shoulder and headed for the coach.

● ● ● ● ●

'No bags, love?' The coach driver grinned at her as he checked her ticket.

Red shook her head.

'You just going down for the day?'

'Kind of,' she nodded.

'Your seat's second from the back on the right-hand side. Window seat.'

'Thanks.'

Red fell into her seat and breathed out slowly. So far, so good. She pulled the locket from beneath her T-shirt and pressed it to her lips. Maybe this afternoon or this time tomorrow she would be handing it over to the Commission.

'Hi there.' A young woman dropped into the seat beside her. 'I'm Cassie.'

'Rose.'

'Nice to meet you, Rose. You going all the way to Melbourne?'

Red nodded.

'I haven't seen you on this coach before. D'you live around here?'

'No, I'm from Sydney.' As soon as she said it, she wished she hadn't. She should have made up a different story, distanced herself from anything to do with Sydney and what had happened there. 'Actually,' she said, 'I was born in Sydney but my family has moved to Melbourne. I've been in Wagga with an auntie.' It was so easy to make up stuff. She could spin a long and complicated yarn. She could make up relations, homes and lives. Did other people do that? Kate? Jazz? Peri? Especially Peri. Was everything he said last night true? Maybe he really had done stuff that got him into serious trouble with the police. Maybe...

Cassie pulled a book out of her bag and turned to Red, 'I hope you don't mind if I read most of this trip. I've got an exam in a week and I have to finish this and write an essay on it. I'm already running late with it.'

'That's OK,' said Red. 'I think I'll sleep. I didn't get much last night.'

She closed her eyes as the coach started up and moved out onto the streets of Wagga.

• • • • •

She opened her eyes from time to time as the coach moved through open country of yellow-brown grassland. Beside her, Cassie was absorbed in her book. Soft music was playing and there was a low buzz of conversation. Red opened her backpack wide and felt in it for the notebook. Her hand brushed the picture book from the library. She half lifted it from her bag and stared at the girl's face. Those eyes stared back at her. She pulled the notebook from its place and the newspapers that she had picked up earlier fell onto the floor. She let her foot rest on the photo.

'I wonder what's happened to those kids,' Cassie leant across to her. 'Can I have a look at what it says? I hope they aren't running around the bush.'

'Mmm.'

'Must have been awful to be in that stuff in Sydney.' She lifted up the paper and then paused. 'You know, this girl looks a lot like you.'

'You reckon?'

'Yes, same eyes, same grin.'

Red looked down at the smiling happy face. It was only three days before. 'No. I think she looks a bit younger.'

'Yeah, possibly. Poor kids. I couldn't bear it if I lost everything, I mean, you wouldn't have any of your precious stuff. You'd hardly even know who you were.'

• • • • •

They swung onto the Hume Highway, heading south for Victoria. Across from them, heading north, was a convoy of army trucks.

'They'd be going up to Sydney to help clean up,' said Cassie. She turned back to her book. Red watched the heavily camouflaged vehicles till the last one disappeared from sight and then picked up the other newspaper, the *Sydney Morning Herald*. The cover page was filled with images of the rescue centre where she and Peri had been. Huge piles of clothing were stacked on trestle tables and boxes of toys lay waiting to be sorted. A single line on the bottom of the page caught her eye: *Melbourne*: *Royal Commission to Close. See page 4.*

She flipped the pages over so quickly that they tore. The Commission couldn't close. She had to get the memory stick to them. Her eyes flicked down over stories from around the nation: a rail strike in Adelaide, a new iron ore deposit in the Pilbara. There, in a small paragraph:

Royal Commissioner Justice John Stanton said yesterday that only two days remained for hearings into accusations of murder, drug trafficking, money laundering and institution-alised police corruption. 'We have almost exhausted the list of witnesses,' the Judge said. 'Some evidence, including police files and company and taxation records, has been lost in the cyclone damage in Sydney. We currently have officers from our team searching for the missing evidence and unless computer backups of these records can be restored, this avenue of inquiry must close.'

Red let the newspaper lie on her lap. Two days. That meant today and tomorrow. 'Cassie,' she said.

'Mmm.'

'What time do we get to Melbourne?'

'I can't remember. Mid-afternoon I think. We stop in a few places on the way.'

Mid-afternoon. Should she wait for Peri and Jazz, or should she try to find the Commission herself?

How could she do that? And if she couldn't find it...?
She pushed that thought from her mind.

Red opened her notebook. She slipped a pen from its place lodged in the spiral backing and turned to the first page. *What I Remember*, she scrawled across the top. She glanced out the window. They were passing through a small town: a single pub with a garage next door, a cafe with two tired-looking chairs on either side of a small table by the window and no one in sight. Then they were back to farmland.

There was a cyclone and Peri found me in the mud and I was saying some name. He reckons it was James Martin. I don't know whose name that is. I didn't know my name or anything. Now I know a few things.

1 *My true name is Rhiannon Chalmers.*
2 *Jazz was my best friend and she broke her arm in Year 5.*
3 *I left with my dad and another man and we went on an aeroplane.*
4 *My dad's name is David and Jazz's mum says I didn't have a mum – or if I did she never met her.*
5 *We were flying to Adelaide and then...*
6 *Now I have Dad's memory stick and I have to get it to the Royal Commission.*
7 *How?*
8 *How?*
9 *How?*

She closed her eyes. She could see the image of her father as he was on screen. She pressed her eyes as tightly closed as she could. Talk to me, Dad. Don't tell me all that stuff about danger. Tell me what to do. Tell me where we went. Tell me where the Commission is. Did I go to school? Where did we live? Did I have friends? Why was I back in Sydney? Who put your stick around my neck? Where are you?

Red sat bolt upright. She'd moved before. With Dad. Never a mum. In the night. Just one suitcase and a raggedy toy dog. Dad saying he was sorry to do this to her. Driving till morning. Where was that? Why? Too many questions. Where are you, Dad?

CHAPTER TEN

THEY STOPPED ON A RISE HIGH ABOVE THE FREEWAY.
Petrol pumps and fast-food cafes sprawled across an
open space cut from the bush. Red followed Cassie
down the aisle of the coach but when they came out
into the sunshine and Cassie headed for food, Red
turned from her and wandered through the carpark.
She wanted silence. She wanted to think of what to do.
Melbourne. She would get there and then what? It was
a big city. The coach station would be much bigger
than in Wagga. She would do what Peri said. She would
wait. There would be lots of seats and she could just
hang about till the next coach came in from Wagga.

Peri would come, and Jazz. They would find someone and ask them where the judge was for the Commission, and then they would go there.

She stopped suddenly. Ahead of her was a fence, then a paddock of dry grass. A light brown horse with a splash of white over its nose stood a few metres from her, its head down, munching grass. At her footsteps it lifted its head and took a step towards the fence.

Red trembled.

There's a horse leaning over the fence. I'm watching it. Dad says go on, pat it on the nose, it won't hurt you but the horse tosses its head up, up and it lifts its lips over teeth as big as teacups and they are dirty yellowy-grey, splashed with black stains and it blows through them making weird flubbery sounds and I turn and run back into the house and I am on my bed and I am crying and crying and crying.

Tears filled Red's eyes. She turned, ran back weaving her way through the cars till she was at the edge of the carpark. She stopped, her chest heaving, and leant against the pole that held up the giant entrance sign. More cars came in off the freeway. She spun around. Where was her coach? A loud blast sounded. That was it. She wiped her eyes and made her way towards it.

'Nearly left you behind, love.' The driver slipped the coach into gear and Red made her way along the aisle and dropped down into her seat. That horse. That is where I was. A place in the country and the horse was next door. Red could feel the cotton doona and the pillow she hugged close to her chest. *Dad is standing in the doorway. Don't be so scared, he is saying. It's only a horse. He can't come in here. Don't be such a chicken.*

'Are you OK?' said Cassie.

Red nodded.

'Do you want some?' She held out a bag of chocolate-covered nuts.

Red took a couple and started to suck on them gratefully.

They were back on the freeway but after about ten minutes the coach slowed.

Red looked at Cassie. The girl shrugged.

The coach stopped, then started and crawled forward, then stopped again.

'What do you think's going on?'

'I don't know,' said Cassie. 'Maybe there's a prang up ahead.'

The stopping and starting continued.

Twenty minutes passed. Red couldn't read, couldn't think. She strained forward in her seat. A long line of cars stretched into the distance.

'This will make us late getting to Melbourne, won't it?' said Red. What time would the Commission close?

'Sure to.' Cassie looked at her watch.

The cars ahead were crawling, crossing three lanes and moving into a single line.

Finally, through the front windscreen of the coach they could see the flashing lights of police vehicles.

'Must be an accident,' said Cassie.

Then there were policemen on the road, going from car to car.

'They're talking to people. They're checking for something,' she said.

Red glanced at the newspapers on the floor. Were they checking for her?

The coach stopped. Two policemen were walking the length of the outside. They pressed their faces to the glass, peering in the windows. Red pushed herself down, low in her seat and opened her notebook.

A young policeman came up and into the coach. He spoke briefly to the driver and then stepped into the aisle.

'This will only take a few minutes,' he said. 'We are conducting a search for three young people from Sydney who are believed to be in the area: two females and one male.' He moved forward, slowly, glancing at the figures in their seats. 'We want them for a number of things, including a theft in Wagga last night. We've been informed that they are heading for Melbourne so we are checking all the coaches on the highway.'

Red flicked her hair forward over her face. Did that make her look different enough?

The policeman was coming closer. He spoke to a boy two seats in front of her. 'Your name, young fella?'

The boy mumbled something. Red gripped her notebook, held her breath.

If he asked her name and she said 'Rose' he would know she was the one who had been at the police station the night before, who had stolen the money. Kate and her mother must have dobbed them in. Why hadn't she given Cassie a different name?

Now he was at the seat in front. Only an old man was there.

Now he was smiling down at Cassie, now looking at Red. She kept her shoulders hunched, her eyes raised only to the wide black belt around his hips.

'You young lady, what's your name?'

Struck dumb. A rabbit in the headlights.

'She's my sister,' said Cassie. 'We're from Melbourne. We're on our way home.'

'Fair enough.' He moved on.

Red held her breath.

The policeman reached the back of the coach. He turned and walked quickly to the front. 'Thank you all. If any of you do see them I would ask you to report that information. Have a pleasant trip.'

Red let out a deep sigh.

'That is you in the paper, isn't it?' said Cassie.

Red nodded.

'What happened to the other two? Your mates?'

'They stayed in Wagga. We had to split up.' She paused. 'Thank you for that.'

'That's OK. It did seem like a bit of overkill. Since when do they stop buses for a theft in Wagga? They'd have to stop every bus, every day. You don't look like a crim.' She laughed. 'We'll be in Kelly country soon.'

'Kelly country?'

'You know, the bushranger. Ned Kelly.'

Red nodded. She didn't have a clue what Cassie was talking about. Why had this girl helped her? So much had happened in the last hour. She wanted to take her mind back to that house in the country, the bed, her father. If she could remember that, then there must be other memories. How could she get to them?

She fixed her mind on herself, lying on the bed. If she could just get that other self to turn over, sit up, look around. What else was in the room? What else was in the house?

Cassie was still talking about the Kelly gang. Red picked up the notebook and stared at the blank page. She started to doodle, quick scribbled lines that took on the shape of a bed.

The coach was back up to full speed. Red glanced at the wide open countryside and then back at her page. What happened next?

She closed her eyes. Stay in that room. There was a bed and a table beside it. There was a lamp on the table. Was there a bookcase like the one in Jazz's room? A computer? A desk? A wardrobe for her clothes? She tried to see them but it felt as though she was imagining these things. How could she tell what was a memory and what wasn't?

She stared at the sheet of paper till her doodles blurred.

• • • • •

We are standing in the kitchen and he is saying that I have to go to school it is a risk but he is not going to wreck my education I have to go. I will not go I am saying you can't make me I don't know anyone I won't have any friends and they will be doing different work and they will all think I am really stupid even though I am not and I am yelling at him not crying this time. You are so smart I am saying you can teach me whatever I have to know. He leans on the table and he says that he doesn't know everything that he can teach me some stuff but we don't have enough books and sure most stuff is online but he has to use the computer for work and we'll talk about it in the morning. I'm not going I say.

And I didn't. He wanted me to but in the end he got lessons from somewhere and I did them on the table while he worked on the computer.

This felt true. A memory. Where had it come from? How could she know this and so little else? She looked back at her list.

10 *We were in the country and I was scared of a horse.*

11 *I didn't want to go to school.*

12 *I knew we were safe but I didn't know what we were safe from.*

• • • • •

How long did they stay there? Why did she end up in the mud in Sydney? She closed her eyes again and let the humming of the coach engine block everything else from her mind.

• • • • •

It was mid-afternoon. The sun was now streaming through Red's window. Farmland had given way to suburban houses.

'How long before we get in to Melbourne?' Red asked.

Cassie looked out the window. 'We're kind of there. Another half hour to the station.' She closed the book she was reading. 'Are you all right? Where are you off to then? What are you going to do?'

Red hesitated. Should she tell her? Cassie had been so kind already. She might help. Should she say 'I have to find the judge who is at the Royal Commission'?

'I'm being picked up by a friend,' said Red. 'If they aren't there, I have to wait for them.'

'It's not too bad a place. They did it up so it's all flashy but you should find somewhere to wait.'

The freeway took them high above city blocks and

then back to street level. The coach turned down further, underneath the huge station and pulled into a bay alongside others. Like pigs lining up for a feed. Where had that thought come from? How did she know that?

'Good luck,' said Cassie as she tugged at a bag above their seats.

'Thanks.' Red waited till the others had left the coach and were gathered around the side where the driver was pulling out suitcases, cardboard boxes tied with yellow twine and huge, thick plastic carrybags.

She wandered up the escalator and through the station, under giant billboards carrying lists of arrivals and departures and flashing notices saying *boarding, cancelled* or *departed*.

People were clustered around drink machines and snack dispensers. Others sprawled on the seats or sat in groups on the floor.

Scuffling noises came from Red's right. She turned to see a young man cowering in front of four policemen.

Red stared at the men, their high black boots, their belts with a baton, a gun, a hand-held computer clipped to them. They each had neat, short hair and their shirts were stretched tight across the muscles of their chests and shoulders. Their sunglasses separated them from everyone: they could see your eyes; you could see nothing of the person behind the shades. They were the biggest men she'd ever seen.

Red's stomach lurched. She had to get away. She ducked into the ladies' toilet, dropped her backpack and turned on the water in the hand-basin hard. She scrubbed and scrubbed at her palms. Her heart was pumping. Why was she so afraid? She'd done nothing wrong. Well, not much, and she would pay Kate back. Her father's words on the memory stick came back to her. *Do not, under any circumstances, allow it to fall into the hands of any other person. Do not take it to the police. Trust no one. I repeat, no one.*

So she couldn't just go up to a policeman and ask him where the Commission was. He might want to know why she wanted to go there, who she wanted to see.

• • • • •

'Are your hands really dirty?' A little kid, her head level with Red's waist, stared up at her.

'Something like that.' Why was she still washing them? Where should she go now? When did the next coach come in from Wagga? Would Peri and Jazz be on it? What if Kate's mum had found them? Or the police?

She stood shaking her hands under the drying machine till not a drop of water was left on her fingers.

Minutes passed. A steady stream of women and girls moved through the washroom. Sometimes Red studied them; sometimes she read the posters, the paper cracked and browning, their edges curling from the wall. They warned of personal safety, health checks and where to get help if you were pregnant.

She should go and check the timetable, see when she could expect Peri and Jazz. She pushed the door open enough to see across the concourse. No police.

Red stepped forward into the station.

The arrivals board flashed yellow signals. The next coach from Wagga was due in two hours. Two hours. Five o'clock. But would it also be searched on the freeway? Would Jazz and Peri be picked up by those police? Should she wait? How to fill in that time? Red wandered past the cafes, the chemist shop and the travel agent. She stopped in front of the newsagent. NATIONAL DAY OF MOURNING. The huge letters, inside a thick black square, filled the billboard. Piles of newspapers were stacked in the window. On one, the front page was filled with images of horrific destruction: in black and white the crumbling facades of once-solid buildings, mountains of rubble that had been homes, schools and businesses. On another the face of a weeping woman, her old body bent, one hand holding tightly to a plastic bag, the other to her walking stick. And the headline: *Lost Everything, Again.*

Her body shaking, Red was suddenly back in Sydney, in the mud, staring at Peri on the table. The name *jaymartinjaymartin* was pounding in her head. She turned away and tried to focus on the men and women pouring through the station but they merged to blurs of colour while she staggered forward. She tried to think of the road and the rolling countryside. Nothing could drive the images of mud from her mind. And the child. She saw again the weeping toddler clinging to the leg of his mother, also weeping at the photos on the board. She'd picked him up and carried him out. Were they back there, waiting, hoping? Red found a spare seat and dropped down onto it, her backpack on her lap. She closed her eyes and clutched the bag to her chest. She couldn't go looking for the Commission. She would just sit here till the Wagga coach came in.

Red sat for a long time. Gradually her mind drifted to the bus, charging down the freeway, the droning of the engines lulling her towards sleep when she felt a tugging on the leg of her shorts. A toddler with tangled hair falling into her eyes, grubby fingers and a grin that filled her face was pulling herself up from the floor. She rested both hands on Red's knee.

'Tylor,' said the woman next to Red. 'Leave the lady alone.'

'She's OK.' Red leant forward. 'Hello Tylor.'

The little girl giggled, clapped her hands and fell backwards.

'Can I pick her up?'

'Sure.'

Red pushed her backpack onto the seat beside her and lifted Tylor onto her lap. The child giggled and grinned. Red felt herself grinning too. 'You're a smiley girl.'

Tylor laughed. Red laughed and felt her body relaxing back against the seat. Had she ever held a baby before? She jiggled her knees so that Tylor bounced up and down.

'I wouldn't do too much of that,' said the mother. 'She's just had lunch. She'll bring it up all over you.' She took a small plastic duck from her bag. 'Here, Tylor.' She squeezed the toy and it made a sound something like a quack. The little girl snatched it and held it close.

'Where are you heading off to?' She turned her attention back to Red.

'Nowhere. I've just arrived. I'm waiting for someone coming in on a coach.'

'Family?'

'No. My best friends.' It felt good saying that. Peri and Jazz. Best friends. Jazz was her oldest friend, Peri her newest. She could have said only friends in the whole world. She pushed that thought away. 'They're on the next coach from Wagga.'

'We're going up to Ballarat,' said the woman. 'To my mum's. It's her birthday tomorrow and she's having a big family party. All her kids, her brothers and sisters. My cousins. There'll be about fifty people there. Some of them haven't met Tylor yet.'

'They'll think she's gorgeous.' Red stroked the little girl's hair. Birthday parties, family, cousins. Would she ever know if that was part of her life? More thoughts to push away.

The afternoon wore on. Tylor and her mother left. Red watched the numbers on the clock tick over. She studied the people around her. She challenged herself not to look at the clock until she had counted four men with tattoos, then three people with pull-along black bags, then five people talking on their phones. If only she had a phone she could call Peri, if only he had one too.

Four-thirty. Maybe the coach would be early. She checked the arrivals board. Bay eleven. She walked slowly across the concourse and down the escalator until she could see the empty bay. Half an hour. Peri and Jazz would be there. They'd jump down from the coach and their eyes would search the crowd and they would see her and grin with relief. They'd work out what to do together. Everything would be all right.

• • • • •

At a quarter past five, the Wagga coach pulled in. Red moved towards it as the doors opened and the driver stepped out. He stood back and waved down the first passengers: two women with children, an old man with a walking stick who stepped carefully and took the driver's arm, a couple who looked the same age as Cassie, more school kids and families.

No Peri. No Jazz.

Red couldn't move. She stared at the crowd gathering bags from the side of the coach. She scanned the group, willing the young man in a black leather jacket to somehow turn into Peri, the girl at his side to be Jazz. Where were they? She wanted to climb onto the coach, to check every seat, under the seats, to find them hiding, teasing her. They would burst out laughing, tricking her. She turned away, cold and empty.

• • • • •

Back in the hall she dropped down on the floor outside one of the cafes. The lights were on now and people were rushing, their briefcases and bags clutched tightly, heading for the trains and buses to take them home. Where would she sleep tonight? In a corner of the room an old man in a long khaki coat was arranging newspapers and a collection of plastic bags stuffed to overflowing with bits of fabric and pages from magazines. His black shoes were torn open at the toe and he kept hitching up his trousers that hung down to the floor over his heels. Red watched him settle down, his head on one of the bags. He drew his knees up and took a beanie out of one of the bags and pulled it down over his eyes.

• • • • •

A cool wind was blowing through the coach station. Red hunched her shoulders, hugging her backpack.

Could she sleep out here? What could she use for a blanket? A young man squatted on the floor beside her.

'I reckon you need company, love.' He held out his hand and Red saw only the thick black grime under his fingernails. She smelt beer breath and looked away.

'No.'

'Don't be like that.'

'Go away. Leave me alone.' She clutched her bag.

He sat down and slid closer. 'Watcha got in there?' Again the grimy hand slid towards her.

'I said go away.'

He tilted his head back and laughed.

She thought again of the horse and the yellow-grey teeth. She pushed herself up and moved towards the warmth of the cafe. He was following her, like a dog on a leash, a few steps behind.

'I'm not going to hurt you,' he said. 'I just want some company.'

Red turned and faced him. 'Please leave me alone.'

He slowly shook his head. 'No way.' He stretched his lips into a sly, leering smile and stepped towards her, his arms outstretched.

Red shuddered, gasped and ran to the ladies' bathroom. She pushed into the furthest cubicle and dropped onto the closed lid of the toilet. How dare he! She could feel her heart thudding in her chest. She should have slapped him or whacked him over the head with her backpack. She leant back and let her eyes float over the writing on the door in front of her. Weird drawings in thick black texta. Tanya loves James. 4ever... Peta Christos is a slut...

She stood up and wrenched the door open. She kicked her bag into the far corner of the washroom. How dare he. And how dare Dad. Why was she here by herself? Why did she have to do this? Where was he? She paced up and down the narrow strip in front of the mirrors. Why her? She bit her lip, felt her whole body tense, every muscle held tight ready to explode. She spun round to stare at her face in the mirror; eyes shadowed and sunken, her mouth a slash across her pale skin. She gripped the handbasin and then lashed out, slapping her image in the glass hard. Blood burst from the torn scabs on her hand. Pain ripped through her fingers and she fell sobbing to the floor.

She blew and sucked on her hand. She should have told Jazz's parents. She should have stayed in Sydney with their family. She would be in a warm bed now with a full belly. They were good people. They couldn't be the ones her father had warned about on the stick. They would have known what to do. She used her good hand to wipe the tears from her cheeks and crawled to where her bag had landed. Dragging it behind her she went into the nearest cubicle and pushed the door shut.

Someone came into the cubicle next to her. Red dropped her head down and saw scarlet stilettos. Then there was flushing and the door opening and closing and the clacking of the shoes to the basins and then out.

Good, the room would be empty.

Red wedged herself into the corner of the cubicle, half lying on her backpack. The tiles were hard and she shifted from her back to her side and then to her other side. That was no more comfortable. She rested her pack on the closed lid of the toilet and pressed her head against that. She felt the rumble and the vibration of trains below her.

She couldn't sleep. She curled herself up into a ball hugging her knees. She rocked herself backwards and forwards. She scratched at a loose thread that hung from the bottom of her shorts, an itchy spot inside her left elbow and a mosquito bite on her left ankle. Above the red lump of the bite was a fading green and yellow bruise. Too old to be from the rocks and the mud. It must have been from before. When? How?

I am in the bathroom and Dad is yelling to me. Come on he's saying hurry up the driver won't wait. We are catching another plane and I am running to where he is but I stumble on the laundry step and I crack my shin against the box of tools. There is a bruise straight away and he wraps some ice in a teatowel because we can't wait there is a plane leaving and we have to catch it because Grandma Chalmers is sick in Sydney and everything is arranged that we will go to her. We may not ever see her again if we don't get there tonight. I don't cry

on the plane but I go on and on about how much it hurts
and he puts his arm across my shoulders and says that
no one ever died from a bruise on their leg.

• • • • •

Did she say something clever back to him? Red
touched the bruise but it no longer hurt. So that was
why they were in Sydney this time. Did they go to her
grandmother? Was she all right? Is that where she was
when the cyclone struck?

Nothing. The trapdoor over the tunnel to her
memory was back.

She unzipped her backpack and took out the
notebook.

13 *We went back to Sydney because my grand-*
mother was sick and Dad wanted to see her.

She put the notebook back and took out the picture
book that she'd taken from the library. In all the time
she had been carrying it around she'd never even
opened it. She made herself as comfortable as she
could on the floor, pressing her back into a corner,
and spread the book in front of her. In the first few
pages the girl was a small figure in a pale grey shawl.
Nothing was written above or below the images. She
was walking through briefly sketched landscapes: a
few houses, trees, tall buildings. Then she was beyond
those images, moving alone through wide open spaces.
The lines that defined her body grew stronger and

stronger. She grew larger and larger as she headed across the white pages. Her shawl, now a black cloak, blew out behind her and ahead of her was a light that she advanced towards, getting closer, ever closer. Red turned to the last page. The simple black lines were gone. The girl was in colour now, dancing with crowds and crowds of people who flocked through city streets. She was smiling, with her arms extended, and all was in colour, glorious colour.

Red picked up the book and, wrapping her arms around it, hugged it tightly to her chest. She must have dozed, because at one point she found that she had slipped away from the corner and was lying on the cold tiles. Through the skylight above her she saw only black sky and rain that streamed against the glass. Her shoulder hurt and she sat up rolling her head and stretching out her arm. She closed the book and pushed it back down into her backpack.

• • • • •

Red went out to the washbasin and splashed cold water on her face. If she wasn't going to sleep she could start thinking and work out what to do. First, she needed to get warm. She found Jazz's jeans in her bag and quickly changed into them. If she made it to the Commission they would look better than her shorts.

She walked up and down in the darkness. What would Peri do? He would work out some way of getting to the judge by making up some lies. He'd tell them to police or to strangers or to anyone who could give directions or give them a lift or help them find out where they had to go. If he didn't have any money or food, he would get them somehow and think nothing of it. And he'd just shrug his shoulders if anyone said he shouldn't.

What would Jazz do? First she would whinge and say she wanted to go home or get help from her mum and dad. Red grinned at that thought. Then she'd want to go online and maybe contact the judge and do it all from a comfortable seat somewhere.

Red stopped, folded her arms and stared at her shadowy form in the mirror. What would I do?

She dropped back down onto the floor, tilted her head back and closed her eyes. What would *I* do?

CHAPTER ELEVEN

RED WOKE TO THE SOUND OF A METAL BUCKET SCRAPING across the tiled floor. Grey morning light seeped through the rain that still spattered the skylight.

'Morning, sunshine.' A stout older woman, her hair pulled back under a bright red scarf, leant on her mop. 'Cow of a day out there. Now why on earth aren't you home with your mum and dad?'

Red pushed her stiff body up from the floor and splashed cold water on her face.

'OK, then. Don't mind me. I'm just the poor sod who has to clean up after you drinking, drug-taking lot.'

'That's not fair. I don't drink. I don't take drugs and I haven't made a mess. You can't even tell I've been here.' Red slung her backpack over her shoulder. 'And I haven't got a mum or a dad.'

'Oops. Sorry, love.' The woman felt in the pocket of her apron and held out a couple of coins. 'Take these. Get yourself something to eat. You look half starved.'

Red shook her head. 'I don't need your money. I have some.' Somewhere was the twenty dollars that Peri had given her. She hadn't spent a cent. Her stomach groaned. She felt suddenly ill with hunger. 'But thank you.'

She headed out onto the open concourse. Around her shops and stalls still had their blinds or shutters drawn but ahead was the bright red and gold neon of the internet cafe.

Red ordered scrambled eggs on toast and a bottle of water and found a seat as far from the door as she could. She sat on the edge, glancing at each person who came in, bought a takeaway coffee and then disappeared.

What would I do? She pulled out her notebook and turned to a blank page.

Find the Royal Commission, she wrote. Then in capital letters: *HOW?????*

She sat staring at the page until a young woman in a black apron delivered her the steaming plate of toast and eggs. Red ate quickly. She couldn't tell lies like

Peri, she wouldn't know what to make up, and she wouldn't be game. She chewed on the last crust of toast and looked around. The far side of the room was lined with computers. Maybe she could google it just like they'd done back at Jazz's place. The Royal Commission, Justice Stanton. Surely somewhere in the files would be an address.

She finished and pushed her plate aside and went to the waiter.

'I want to go on the computer.'

'No can do.'

'Why?'

'The server's got some problem. We've been offline since yesterday. Did you want to check your email?'

'No. I just want to look up something.'

'Can I help?'

Red paused. 'There's this Royal Commission on here and I want to know where it is.'

The young woman laughed. 'Don't ask me, love. I'm from Bendigo. I've only been in Melbourne for a week. I don't know where anything is. You'll have to ask someone at the information desk.'

Red paid and went out onto the concourse. Against the far wall, the old man's beanie-covered head poked out of the bundle of newspapers and rags. Black-suited businessmen and women, their dripping umbrellas tucked under their arms, strode quickly past him, not seeing.

Would Peri and Jazz come in on the next coach? Red pushed that thought away. She couldn't wait. Today was the last day. She would find the Commission on her own.

The shutters of the information centre were open, the lights were on and stands with brochures and posters spilled out onto the concourse. A policeman and a security guard stood talking at the entrance under a poster: *National Gallery of Victoria* read the huge print over an image of a young woman in old-fashioned clothes, lying in a hammock with a small child on her lap. Red thought of Tylor the giggling, smiley little girl and wondered where she was now.

Red took a deep breath, fixed her eyes on the desk inside and walked straight past the men.

'I need to find the Stanton Royal Commission,' she said in a soft voice.

The woman frowned. 'Pardon?'

'The Royal Commission, the one that's on here in Melbourne.'

The woman turned to the curtained rear of the office and called out in a loud voice. 'Royal Commission, Matthew? D'you know where that is?'

Red glanced at the men in the doorway. Had they heard? They made no movement.

Matthew came through from the back. 'I reckon your best bet would be to go up to William Street where it joins onto Lonsdale Street. There's a whole complex up there: the Supreme Court, the Family Court and a whole bunch of others. I think there's even the High Court of Australia. Yes, that's probably the one you want.'

He picked up a brochure with a map of the city and took a red pen. 'You go out the door here to get to Bourke Street, go along there till you get to William Street and turn left. It'll take you ten minutes, max.' He marked the spot on the map and handed it to her.

• • • • •

Red stood at the bus station exit. The Supreme Court. That sounded like the most important one. There would be judges there. Maybe even the Commission. They would know. She could ask there. Ten minutes. If that man was right she might meet the Judge in ten minutes.

She pulled a newspaper from a rubbish bin and held it over her head. Rain dripped down over her shoulders.

What if the Commission wasn't at the Court? What if it was but no one would see her? What if it was there but they knew nothing of her father and whatever was on the memory stick? What if they wouldn't let her in? What if you have to be dressed up for court? She shook her head. Stop it. You have got this far. You are nearly there.

She was swept along by the crowds heading out of the station. Water splashed up from the cars that raced past. More droplets ran from the sodden newspaper down her arms and onto her face. At the Bourke Street corner she tossed the paper into a bin and stood pressed between men and women in black suits waiting for the green light to cross.

• • • • •

Red stood in the shelter of a bus stop across the road from the court. Dark stone base, paler walls of huge stone blocks and above them a dome. Policemen on the footpath, policemen by the doors. She felt suddenly smaller than she had ever felt before. She lifted the memory stick from beneath her shirt and put it to her lips. 'Nearly there,' she whispered, 'nearly there.'

After fifteen minutes she was still standing and staring, watching individuals arrive and enter the building.

A tram stopped in the middle of the street and about a dozen students in school uniform poured across the road to where Red stood. They gathered around their teacher.

'This is a rare opportunity,' she said. 'Even though this is the last day of the Royal Commission, we are still able to attend and listen to the judge's summing up.' She smiled broadly. 'You can tell your children you were there at the most significant inquiry into organised crime in the country.'

Red moved a little closer. She turned her head away as if studying the cracks in the concrete wall behind her, while straining to hear every word.

'When we get into the court building I want you all to go to the toilet if you feel the need. No one will be allowed out of the room to wander around without me. Remember, you are on your best behaviour, representing your school. No nonsense, now. And we'll follow up tomorrow with a brief test on all that happens today. OK. Any questions?'

They started across the road. Red followed. The policemen took no notice as they went up a flight of steps and into a huge room with a shiny marble floor and dark panelled walls. One by one they placed their backpacks on the belt of the X-ray machine. Then they stepped forward through the frame that X-rayed them. A sound buzzed and the boy in front of Red was called over to the security man. He pointed to the boy's boots and Red slipped past him as he bent to take them off.

She followed a group of girls into the ladies' room. She stood with her head under the hand-dryer, flicking water from her damp hair.

'This is going to be really boring,' said one girl.

'Better than school,' said another. She had taken a mascara wand from her pocket and was carefully applying it to her lashes.

'D'you reckon they'll have prisoners in a dock, like on television?'

'Nah. It's not a trial. They'll just be talking about murders and stuff like that. My mum said it's all about the mob that brings in the heroin and the coke and other drugs too. And then they pay off some of the cops so they don't get picked up and charged. Only sometimes it all goes wrong and people get murdered.'

'Who gets murdered?'

'I don't know. Drug dealers I s'pose.' Mascara Girl glared at Red. 'Watcha looking at?'

'Nothing.' *Already some attempts have been made on my life…* She pushed the thought from her mind and followed the girls out of the room.

• • • • •

Red joined a group of the students in a lift and pressed herself against the far wall. One or two of them looked at her but said nothing.

• • • • •

When they stepped out of the lift on the sixth floor they were met by a security guard in a grey uniform. After a brief conversation with the teacher, he addressed the group.

'Leave your backpacks here. Keep your mouths shut, nod to the bench when you step inside and sit in the back rows. There're plenty of seats. It's a boring day for you today.' He laughed. 'No crooks.'

'What's the bench?' Red heard someone whispering.

'The judge up the front.'

'Can I take my notebook?' Red wasn't sure why she said that.

He nodded.

The room was smaller than Red expected. She forgot about the other students around her. She nodded at the old man sitting at the far end of the room on a raised platform. He didn't acknowledge her. He didn't acknowledge anyone. Thick piles of papers and a laptop almost hid him from view. In front of him were two women, facing out into the room, and on rows of chairs facing them and the judge were about a dozen other men and women.

'Counsel,' said the judge, and a woman from the front row stood up and began to speak. Red glanced along the back row. One man at the far end was scribbling quickly in a notebook so Red opened her notebook and took up her pen.

What should she write? The words being spoken meant nothing. Some words she knew...evidence ...surveillance...police officer...witnesses...but she got lost in the complicated way that the woman spoke. Sometimes her voice was soft and Red found her mind drifting to thoughts of Peri and Jazz. Where were they? Would they be on a coach today? Should she go back to the station after she delivered the memory stick to the judge? And if they weren't on the coach, did that mean they had been picked up by the police?

She looked up at the judge. He had taken off his glasses and he was staring intently at the speaker. Although his hair was white, his eyebrows were thick and black and they almost met in the middle of his forehead. Would she dare to go up to him when she got the chance? They must stop for lunch or something like that. What would she say? I've got something for you, from my father. Would he believe her or would he call the security guard and throw her out of the room? Would it be better to give it to one of the others? Maybe the women sitting in front of him, or the one who was speaking.

She was huge: her long grey hair was gathered in a pile on top of her head and as she spoke she waved her arms so the sleeves and front panels of her jacket billowed around her. Her lips were bright scarlet and her voice was angry, deep and husky. She frowned and none of the students around Red moved a muscle. Red felt she could never approach her.

She spoke on and on.

Red felt her head dropping forward and her eyes closing. She struggled to stay alert. She had to concentrate, to listen. Something might be said of her father.

More talk of things she didn't understand…phone tapping…listening devices…witness protection.

At that Red sat up. *Witness protection.* That was her. Her and her father.

'A number of our investigators and witnesses,' said the woman, 'have been in protection for some time, and there is one in particular that I want to speak about.'

Her father. It must mean her father. Red sat forward, on the edge of her seat. The woman stopped. She looked to the back of the room. The security man had come in. He moved forward quickly to the judge's platform and spoke to him. The judge nodded, removed his glasses and stood up.

The woman was looking to him for some direction. He indicated he wanted to speak to her and for a moment their two heads were bent together and the room was silent. Then he lifted up his hand.

'I have just been informed,' he said, placing his glasses in the top pocket of his jacket, 'that there has been a threat to this building. I would ask you all to stand and to leave as quickly as possible. This court is adjourned until further notice.'

'Bomb scare...bomb scare,' nervous laughter. The whisper went from one student to another. They ignored their teacher and scrambled to their feet and headed for the door.

Red stood on her toes and looked towards the bench. The judge was still there.

Now was her chance.

'Hey, you. Where are you going?' The security guard was in front of her. A policeman had joined him.

'I have something for the judge.'

'No you don't. You're to leave the building immediately. All your mates have gone.'

The room was almost empty. The security guard grabbed Red's arm and swung her around. The policeman grabbed her other arm. They moved quickly for the door. Red struggled, turned her head. The huge grey-haired woman was walking past the judge's bench to a side door. The judge had gone.

'Help!' screamed Red. 'Help!' She kicked the policeman hard in the shins and drove her elbow into the security man's stomach.

'Help!'

The men stopped pushing her. The grey-haired woman turned to look.

Red shook herself free of the security guard but the policeman's fingers still dug into her arm.

'Help me,' she called to the woman. 'I have something for the judge.'

'You have to leave the building. There's a bomb scare.'

'I know, but I've got something for the judge.' She was feeling around her neck for the memory stick. Her fingers locked on the cord.

'What? You mean Judge Stanton?' The woman came towards her.

'Yes.'

'And you are?'

'Red. No. That's what I'm called. Or Rose. But really I think my name is, my name is Rhiannon Chalmers.'

The woman's mouth dropped open, then spread into an enormous grin. 'Am I pleased to meet you.' She held her arms out wide and then placed both her hands on Red's shoulders. 'I'm Jane Martin.'

CHAPTER TWELVE

JAYMARTINJAYMARTINJAYMARTIN.

I am on the balcony at Grandma's flat. His hands are around my neck. Dad's hands. You have to run he is saying. Not saying, screaming. The wind flings his words into the rain. It's pelting sideways into us. Like bullets. It stings my cheeks, my arms, my legs. I'll stay with Grandma, he says. I can't leave her. We'll be all right. But you have to run. Why do I have to go, I am screaming too. Why? The seawater's coming in. There's no power, no phone we may not get help. I can't leave. You have to. You have to wear this around your neck. Don't lose it. You have to be brave and run as fast and as far as you

can. This has to go to the Commissioners in Melbourne,
OK? Melbourne. He is wrapping me in his arms. His
beard is brushing my cheek. He's soaking wet too. His
lips are in my hair. My brave girl. Give it to Jane Martin.
Say that name again. Jane Martin.

I am shivering. Sopping wet. Crying. I can't go. You
must. Say the name again. Jane Martin. Jane Martin.
Jane Martin.

● ● ● ● ●

'Rhiannon? Rose? Red? Are you all right? You look like
you've seen a ghost.'

'Just call me Red.'

'We have to get out of here.' She nodded to the men,
'I'll take care of her. We'd better all leave the building.'

Red followed her through the door and along the
corridor to the lift. She took the cord from her neck
and passed it to Jane. 'He said to give you this. It's all
on the stick. Stuff he recorded.'

She could see him; really see him, sitting at his
computer late into the night. She would come out into
the room when she'd woken up and she was scared of
the dark and he would give her a hug and say stay out
here with me and she'd sit beside him while he tapped
away.

'I think I know what's on it.' Jane closed her hand
around the memory stick. 'This is the evidence that's
going to convict a lot of people. He's been a very brave

man finding out all this. And you're a very brave girl getting it to us.'

More memories were coming back. Like waves, not drifting in but crashing, hard on the soft sand. She was running from the flat, leaving him, leaving Grandma still in bed, her eyes closed, wisps of hair loose on the pillow, her wrinkled hands still on the edge of the doona. She was not saying goodbye, the name Jane Martin, *jaymartin,* the pelting rain, the water coming up behind her, the small waves splashing her feet then bigger ones and bigger till she could not stand but was stumbling and was picked up and tossed and was rolling around in the mud and the sand... 'Where is he?' she said. 'Where?'

'We're not sure. We've been contacted by a hospital in Sydney and we've sent someone just today to check and see if it is David and if he's all right. That's what I was about to say when we were told to close the court.'

He would be all right. He must be all right.

They were now at the ground level of the building. They joined others moving out across the road. Policemen were everywhere: lining the footpath, ushering crowds away from the building, directing traffic. Red wanted to grin, to dance in front of them, to call on them to catch her now, but Jane was asking her more questions.

'Now, where are you staying in Melbourne? Who did you come here with?'

Red shook her head. 'Nowhere. No one.'

Jane gaped. 'You came here from Sydney on your own?'

Red nodded. She was suddenly lighter. She was OK. Dad was probably OK. With any luck Peri and Jazz were OK too. She would know everything sooner or later.

More thoughts were coming into her head; she was walking with Dad from Bronte to Bondi. Hundreds of people were walking there, looking at the sculptures set up on the sand and on the rocks and even in the water. Her favourite was a group of tiny shapes like insects made of a thin red wire while he preferred a huge solid shape of rock on the grass above the beach. He bought her a raspberry and blueberry ice cream at the shop and he had one too. When they had finished they poked their tongues out to compare the colour.

● ● ● ● ●

Moments and people were fighting their way into her mind. Red felt a door was opening. Her kindergarten teacher who gave stickers of gold kangaroos when everyone else gave stars…the special student teacher in Year Three who came from Samoa and taught them dancing…drawing pictures on the plaster Jazz wore when she broke her arm…living in the farmhouse in South Australia after the flight to Adelaide and Dad dancing in the kitchen to the songs on the radio. Come on, no one can see you he'd say, and she always said no, you are embarrassing and he'd laugh and then she'd laugh and they'd collapse, giggling, on the floor together.

Jane was talking on her phone. When she had finished she turned to Red. 'We're abandoning the court for the day. The judge has gone back to his chambers and I am going to take the rest of the day off and spend it with you. What would you like to do?'

'I need to know about Dad. And about Peri and Jazz.'

'Who are they?'

'It's a long story but I wouldn't be here without them.'

Jane nodded. 'Let's go and get something to eat. I'll follow up about your dad and you probably need some more clothes. We can go shopping and figure out what to do next. And,' she put her arm across Red's shoulders, 'I want to hear everything about what happened, how you managed to get here.'

• • • • •

An hour later they were sitting in a restaurant, their plates empty. Red was telling the story of Peri's food scavenging in Wagga. She had just reached the part where the boys came screaming down the lane when Jane's phone rang.

'Yes,' she said. 'This is Jane.' A smile filled her face. 'Am I glad to hear from you,' she said. 'That's right.

She's a fabulous girl and she's right here. I'll put her on.' She grinned at Red. 'Your father,' she mouthed as she passed the phone.

Red took it, her hand shaking. 'G'day Dad,' she said.

• • • • •

TWO DAYS LATER

Red stared from the plane as it flew up the coast. She could not take her eyes from the roads, the houses and the scattered buildings, as crumpled as paper screwed up in a giant's hand. Mud and broken trees were strewn inland for hundreds of metres. Then they were over Sydney, turning west to land at a military airport kilometres in from the coast.

'I've arranged for us to stay in a hotel,' said Jane. 'But if you want to go back to where you stayed before, with Jazz's family, I can fix that.'

Red wasn't sure. It all felt so far away. Six days since the cyclone but it seemed like weeks and weeks. Was she the same person? Would she be friends with Jazz? And what about Peri?

'I just want to go to the hospital and see Dad.'

• • • • •

'The building collapsed.' Her dad shrugged and then winced with the pain. One arm was in plaster and thick bandages were wound around his head. Red sat in the chair by the bed, not saying anything. It was enough to look, to take in the face, familiar now. She knew this face, this man and she knew herself.

'I got hit on the head and was out of it for quite a while, ages in fact. There was a fellow who lived a block away. His place was still standing and he didn't leave but he got a few other blokes together and they came through the wreck of ours and a couple of other places and they found a whole bunch of people, including me. If it hadn't been for them...'

'And Grandma?'

Her father shook his head. 'She was asleep when you left, unconscious maybe. She was so close to the end. When the building went down she'd not have known. I tell myself that. It is some consolation.'

'But where is she...her body I mean.'

He shook his head. 'Not recovered. Probably washed away. She's one of the hundreds.'

Red reached over and took his hand. Being with him here made it all real. She had done as he had asked on the memory stick. She had gone to Melbourne to deliver it and now she was back.

• • • • •

Later, back at Jazz's house, sleeping in her room, sitting on the verandah as they had done before, it was as if the whole trip was a dream. It hadn't really happened.

Jazz and her parents welcomed her back with hugs and smiles and almost no questions but Red felt uneasy. She didn't belong there. Peri was the same.

'I'm not staying,' he said, when he was alone in the yard with her. 'I only waited here to see that you were all right and then I'm off.'

'Why? Where will you go?'

'I'll be OK. Don't you worry, but,' he hesitated, 'there's something I want to tell you. I don't know why but …' He turned away from her. 'You know how … when we were at Kate's place and I told you all that stuff about Mum dying and Kelly and Dad and his girlfriend.' He couldn't look at Red. He flopped on the lawn and started tearing small bits of grass into tiny pieces. She didn't know what to say.

'Well, none of that's true. I made it all up. We did live on a farm, the horse bit's true, but when Dad lost his job managing the place, in the drought, we moved into town. They're both drinkers, Mum and Dad, and when he gets blind he gets really aggro and he lashes out. I've got the scars to prove it. He hit her and he hit me, so I left.'

'You mean there never was a car accident?'

'No.'

'And the little sister, Kelly?'

Peri shook his head. 'Just me,' he said. 'What I told you is a better story than the true one.'

'Whew. I don't know what to believe.'

'You can believe this. I'm not making anything up to you any more. The cops? Maybe.' He grinned.

Red flopped forward on the grass beside him. The sun was warm on her back. 'Do you remember the first time we met?' she said.

''Course.'

'You whacked me.'

'Sorry.'

'Twice. I thought you were really horrible.'

'Thanks for the compliment.'

'But you're not. And Dad said he wants to say thank you to you too, when you meet him, for helping me get to Melbourne, I mean.'

Peri didn't answer.

Red kept looking down at the neatly mown grass. 'Me too.'

'What?'

'Thank you.'

'That's OK.' He rolled away from her to lie on his back, stretching his body out to the sun, his eyes closed. 'It was good fun,' he said. 'Better than hanging around here.'

●　●　●　●　●

When Jazz joined them, the subject changed to the day Red had left them in Wagga.

'It was all right for a while,' said Peri. 'We hung out at the river but we got a bit sick of that and we went back up to the station to get the next bus for Melbourne. Kate was there with that young cop – the one who bandaged me up the night before. They were interviewing the staff and we walked right into it.'

'Dad flew down and picked us up,' said Jazz. 'He was seriously pissed off when we told him the whole story. He reckoned he knew all about the commission and he'd been working on it before the cyclone. He said he couldn't believe that we didn't trust him; he could have helped us and all. He didn't know about your dad, though.'

Red listened.

'It's so good to be back home,' said Jazz. 'And this is going to be the best story to tell all my friends when we get back to school. They can be your friends too. And you can decide if you're going to be Rhiannon again or if you're going to be Rose, like when we were in Wagga, or Ruby, like when you put that note up on the board. We can play tricks on them and use different names at different times. We'll be in the same class and we can sit together and do stuff just like we used to in Year Five. It's going to be so cool.'

Red didn't reply. She pressed her hand against her chest and felt the cool metal of the memory stick on her skin. Jane had given it back to her after everything was cleaned off it. 'It's yours, to keep,' she said, 'to remember.'

• • • • •

There will be school but not with Jazz. Dad said they would talk about it when he felt better. 'Not Sydney,' he said when she started to ask him. 'Maybe Melbourne, maybe somewhere else.'

Tomorrow they will talk about and plan it together. Peri too. He will come with her and they will sit in the sun in the hospital garden and Dad will promise to fix it with Peri's mum and dad and he will say 'You kids are so amazing. You have grown so much, Rhiannon.' And she will shake her head and say 'I'm not Rhiannon, Dad, or Rose, and not Ruby, not now, not any more. I'm Red.'

LIBBY GLEESON is an acclaimed and much-loved author
of well over 30 books for children and teenagers. Her books
have been shortlisted for Children's Book Council awards
thirteen times and she has won three times.

Libby has been a teacher and lecturer, and is actively
involved in writers' organisations. In 2007 she was made
Member of the Order of Australia (AM) for services
to literature and literacy education, and in 2012 she
was awarded the Dromkeen Medal.

You can find Libby's website at www.libbygleeson.com.au

• • • • •

You might also enjoy Libby Gleeson's
previous novel, *Mahtab's Story*
Mahtab and her family are forced to leave their home
in Herat and journey secretly through the rocky mountains
to Pakistan, and then to faraway Australia. Will they ever
be reunited with their father? Will they ever find a home?